CABIN BOY

HIS PIRATICAL HAREM - BOOK ONE

DRAKE LAMARQUE

GREY KELPIE STUDIO

ISBN paperback edition 978-0-473-49421-6

Cover by Sarah Loch of Purple Dragon Design

www.purpledragondesign.com

Printed in United States of America via Kindle Direct Publishing

Published by Grey Kelpie Studio

Visit Drake online:

https://www.facebook.com/drake.lamarque.3

https://twitter.com/DrakeLamarque

Facebook reader's group

CHAPTER ONE - IN WHICH WE MEET GIDEON, AND A CAT

Kingston, Jamaica - May, 1720

ather didn't like it when I visited the markets - he said it was common - but I loved everything about them. The huge variety of people from all over the world, visiting on their ships to trade or find something a little more fun.

I could sometimes spend hours simply watching the people and wondering at who they were or why they might be there.

I loved the food, and the things people brought from far away. The barrels of spices, full of the scents of the far East or deepest India. All intoxicating and alluring. Not like the food Father had served back home - all boiled cabbages, roasted meats - dull English food he preferred as it reminded him of home.

I passed a stall run by a sea witch, her hair long and flowing down her back, almost seaweed green in the bright afternoon sunlight. She was selling charms, woven bracelets and necklaces with shells and pieces of sea glass in them. I didn't meet her eyes as I looked over the stall, I didn't want her to see my soul and be able to control me, and I had no need for any of her wares. They would keep a sailor alive in a storm, or protect them from drowning should they fall in - geegaws like that sold very well in port.

Then there were rows of stalls of clothes and fabrics from all over the world. My eye was drawn mostly to the wares of Europe and Africa, the colours and patterns all so varied and beautiful. I lingered at the sight of a long full dress with curious puffed sleeves and a cinched-in waist. Absolutely stunning. I idly wondered what it would feel like to wear such a confection, but of course, that was a dream that could never be. *Shameful thing to imagine*, I heard Father's voice in my head.

Then I saw the people who brought penny press novels from England. Father especially didn't approve of novels.

Ridiculous stories written for serving girls, and idle youths, full of strange fancies and poor morals.

Definitely not appropriate for a young man of means, like myself. He only read treatises on tactics, or Naval history. The only books he'd ever given me covered those subjects, or a particularly boring book about etiquette.

If I saw something I hadn't read in the market, I had to buy it. Those stories were my escape - the high romance, the dashing adventures, the incredible characters. I spent hours reading and re-reading them in my room or in the garden, and the market was the only place to purchase them.

On this particular afternoon the sun was hot, the air smelled of salt spray, fresh bananas and woodsmoke from cooking fires. I bought a couple of hot cassava cakes, fresh off the griddle and some jerked fish to eat on the walk back up the hill to my house, but I wasn't in any rush to get there.

Instead, I took the long way back, dawdling close to the wharves to look at the ships docked in the marinas. Idly, I gazed at them, wondering where they'd come from or where they were going to.

Around half the ships in port were English naval vessels, maybe a quarter were trading ships and the remainder were fishing boats. I didn't pay much attention to the fishing boats, and only a little more to the Navy. Some of the men in the Navy were exceptionally good looking, especially in their formal uniforms, but my own failed Naval career was still a sore point for me, so I forced myself not to spend time admiring them. Best to look away.

No, I much preferred to look at the trading ships and imagine the strange places they could have come from. Had they journeyed a long way? Had they seen any sea monsters or mermaids on their travels? In ten or so months I'd spent in the Navy, I'd never seen anything interesting at all. Not even dolphins - and they were supposed to be attracted to the waves at the bow of a ship - a common sight for sailors.

As I wandered, a ship was coming in to dock. It was a beautiful, green painted vessel with two masts, a fine jutting bowsprit and a figurehead of a horse rearing. Well, the top part of it was a horse, it's front hooves carved to look as if it were pawing the air, the bottom part of it was a fish tail.

I could just make out the name of the ship, painted in bold gold "The Grey Kelpie."

I stopped and leaned against a wall to watch as the boat was moored, rope lashing to the bollards, and a gangplank set to the wharf. The first thing to use the gangplank was a cat - black with wide shoulders and a large head. It walked confidently down the plank, sprung neatly onto the wharf and paused to sniff the air before walking straight towards me.

I smiled at it, ships cats were invaluable. The last thing you wanted was rats in your food stores, and yet they always seemed to turn up. A ship's cat would eat his catches and was generally said to be good luck. It was unusual to see a black ship's cat. As generally witch's cats were black. He came trotting right up to my feet, sat down on his haunches and looked up at me expectantly. His eyes were large and the deep seaweed green you get around a coral reef.

"Hello," I said. I leaned down to scratch between his ears, and he yowled at me in a distinctly demanding manner. Oh, right, he could probably smell the fish I'd bought... well, I wouldn't miss a little bit of it.

I pulled the package out of my pocket and unwrapped the waxed paper, breaking off a piece of fish. I crouched to offer it to him with my fingers and realised he was a fighter - there was a ragged scar across the bridge of his nose, and his ear was missing a piece. As he happily ate the fish out of my hand I realised he had another scar just above his left eye.

"Scrapper, are you?" I asked him, petting along his back as he ate. He purred, a loud, rumbly sort of purr and licked my fingers clean. He looked up at me, expecting more.

I'm a soft touch, so I gave him another piece of fish and he purred even louder. I chuckled to myself. Then a shadow fell over the both of us.

Close behind the cat there was a fine pair of boots. Tall and black. I looked up again to see an impressive looking gentleman. No, impressive didn't even start to describe him. He seemed to be about seven feet tall and three feet across at the shoulders.

He wore a grey military style waistcoat, the kind favoured by privateers, unfastened over a white shirt and a long grey scarf tied loosely so it hung down over his shirt. The sunshine behind him largely cast his face in shadow, making it hard to see details. I stood up quickly, brushing off my hands. The cat yowled in protest.

"You don't have to give him anything, you know," the man said, a laugh in his voice. "Zebulon here is plenty well fed. He has all the rats on the ship to eat and besides that he gets scraps off the crew."

"Oh, I'm sorry," I said. I felt ridiculous, feeding my fish to a cat just because he sat in front of me.

The man smiled and my heart sped up. He was gorgeous. His skin colour was tawny enough to suggest Pacific Island blood and I knew that if Father were to somehow see me talking to him, he'd have severe words for me.

He had piercing green eyes and a dimple in his cheek. He had his share of scars too, I realised, the most obvious being a diagonal one across his right cheek. I suspected his well tended moustache and goatee hid another couple.

"That's all right, lad, just don't let him tell you he's starving, because it's a lie." He laughed again and shook his head. His hair was long, wavy, dark brown, dark enough to look almost black. He wore it out although it went past his shoulders. He looked like the pirate hero of one of my favourite novels. I'd be seeing him in my dreams, for sure.

I had the wild notion that I should introduce myself to him, but then I realised I was being ridiculous again. The man was likely a privateer or a trader, he had no interest in me besides teasing me for feeding a cat that didn't need it. And it wasn't at all appropriate to go around introducing myself to mercenaries or traders.

Zeb the cat twined himself around my legs and mewed prettily, no doubt thinking that if he was endearing I'd reward him with more fish. He was such a big cat that he actually shoved me a little when he rubbed against my calves.

"Right, of course," I said, finally. "Won't happen again."

The man laughed once more and walked away, heading towards a tavern I guessed.

"No more fish," I said to the cat, embarrassed. He yowled at me and my heart twisted. *Oh, what was the harm?*

I unwrapped the fish I'd been giving him and set it on the cobbles. "Go on, eat it all, Zeb," I said.

CHAPTER TWO - IN WHICH GIDEON
RECEIVES AN ORDER

I hesitated before knocking on the door to my father's study. I'd been summoned. I had to go in, but I didn't want to. I was fairly certain I knew what Father was going to say, and I didn't want to hear it. I wanted to keep on doing what I had been doing - very little.

But Father wanted an heir, and that meant one thing - I had to find a girl.

The idea wasn't exactly repulsive, only every girl I'd ever danced with, every girl Father had tried to set me up with before, hadn't impressed me.

I've been to so many balls, so many dances, with so many girls. I felt like I had enough experience to know for sure...

Father showed me beautiful girls, who were well bred, came from money. And, of course, likely to give a male heir - according to Father anyway. I did all the right things. I danced with them at the parties, I brought them drinks, I even took some of them for walks out in the garden or to take the night time air out on the deck.

But the fact is, even though I knew it was all the right

trappings and atmosphere for romance and the girls were doing the absolute best to be charming, it didn't work. I didn't like them in *that* way.

They were lovely girls and I didn't mind being friends with them, or spending an evening talking and laughing, but I never felt any kind of stirring of the heart like I've read in romance novels.

And I've read a lot of romance stories, I know how it's supposed to go. When you meet the one you're destined to be with your heart flutters, your words stutter and you're full of a sense of happiness you've never before known. None of that happened with any of those girls.

So, there was something really wrong with me, something I couldn't ever tell Father about *but... perhaps I'm going to have to.* He's going to tell me that I have to choose a girl and get married.

Finally, I raised my hand, knocked on his door and called out "Father?"

Inside I could hear his chair being pushed back from his desk and his voice rang out.

"Enter, Gideon."

I pushed the door open and made my way inside. I don't like looking at my father in the eyes so I focused on his desk instead. *Coward.*

Governor Keene - my Father - had a very grand study. It had one wall of full-length windows, looking out over the garden, which allowed the scents of flowers in. Or they would if he ever left them open. Beyond the garden, one could see the Port Royal Harbour and the ships coming and going.

The opposite wall was a recessed bookcase. The middle two shelves were lined with books on military strategy from

England, the rest of the shelves were full of mementos of his glory days in the Royal Navy.

He had a collection of terrifying demon masks from Japan which appeared regularly in my childhood nightmares, vases and carpets from Persia and many other strange and fascinating things.

The study was dominated though, by his desk. A gigantic thing of dark mahogany, it seemed to make him seem larger than life. And he was already a tall, imposing man.

The desk was at the far end of the room to the door, so when entering the room you had to approach him at his desk. This gave him a long time to look you over, watch you, and most importantly judge you. I made my way towards him with a troubled heart and leaden feet.

There was a carved wooden chair on my side of the desk, no doubt for me to sit in and be judged further.

"You wanted to see me, Father?"

"Yes, Gideon, please sit down. I want to talk to you about your future. As you know I wish for you to take over my commission here in Kingston. In order to do that you will need to find a wife."

Father was Governor of Kingston, and he had been commissioned that role from the King himself, back in London. We'd moved out here when I was a babe in arms, and my mother used to tell me stories about how awful the voyage had been.

Mother, what would you want of me?

Father didn't even have a portrait of Mother in the study.

"I have royal approval to give this job directly to you when I retire, despite you not having served in the Navy for more than a year."

I looked away, embarrassed. The Navy hadn't been kind or easy and I didn't like to think of it. I stifled a sigh. It wouldn't do for Father to notice me sighing and I had enough practice of hiding it over the years. I just looked at him blankly instead.

"Well?" I looked up at his face then, he was looking at me expectantly. "What have you got to say for yourself, Gideon?"

"A wife, Father?" I said, meekly. I estimated that playing innocent would save me time - probably not a lot of time - but it was worth trying anyway. What I really wanted to do was scream 'I don't want a wife, Father, I want to be left alone!' But I knew that wouldn't sit well with him. And in fact might get me beaten or turned out.

"Yes, Gideon, a wife." My father shook his head. Again, this was a very familiar reaction. Father had been shaking his head at me for as long as I could remember. I was used to it.

Constant disappointment.

"Honestly, it's as if you're being deliberately stupid to bait me."

"I'm sorry, Father," I said. "A wife, of course."

"I shall hold three more dances," he said. "By the end of the third one you will have chosen a suitable girl. Lord knows, you've seen plenty already, but were your mother alive she would go easy on you, I have decided to do the same. Three dances to make your decision, do you understand?"

Three dances and choose your partner for life? Father's definition of going easy on me was nothing like what I imagined Mother would do.

My heart sank into my stomach, three dances. That didn't give me a lot of time before my fate was sealed.

"When will these dances be, Father?" I asked. My heart started to race, as if I were taking part in a running race.

"The first is tomorrow, the next is Saturday and then the third will be the Tuesday following."

Today was Wednesday, meaning I only had what? Six days? Less than a week? That was ridiculous. Father must believe that I already had a certain girl in mind, surely. Or maybe he didn't care if I actually loved the girl or not. Maybe he just wanted me to find a girl to marry and churn out babies and to Hell with my happiness?

That did seem to be the most likely answer.

I licked my lips. A part of me wanted very much to deny his orders, to explain to him that I felt no kind of romantic affection for women and the idea of lying with one in order to create a child was somewhat repugnant to me. But a larger part of me was afraid of my father. He had never held back from beating me when I defied him, and even though I was now twenty years old, I doubted he would hold back from doing it now.

Coward, the voice in my head said again. *You're a no-good coward, just do everything he says. Go to the dance, pick a girl, get married. You're worthless anyway.*

I nodded my head and gave a shallow bow. "Yes, Father. I understand what you wish of me," I said. It wasn't exactly a 'yes, sir, I'll do it,' but Father didn't notice.

"Good boy, Gideon," he said. "You may go. I believe your mother would be proud of you."

Father never spoke much of Mother, except... it was approaching the anniversary of her death by Scarlet Fever. I had been thinking of her often as well.

I left the room, careful not to slam the door behind me, for that would anger Father for sure, and went to my rooms, feeling hopeless.

CHAPTER THREE - IN WHICH GIDEON
MAKES A DECISION

My suite was on the opposite side of the house to Father's study, and a floor up. I had a view over the city. I usually kept the diaphanous green curtains drawn, as too much sun in the room made it unbearably hot.

What am I going to I do?

I lay on my bed, pulled the coverlet over my face and groaned as loud as I dared. What were my choices? Do as Father desired, go to three dances, pick a girl, marry and have babies?

Should I run away?

Dress as a woman and book myself into a finishing school? No, ridiculous. But I felt the need to do something. Maybe running away was the best plan?

But I couldn't overthink it, because if I thought about this too long or too hard I'd talk myself out of it. There was a whole world out there, and if I could get on a boat and off Jamaica, Father wouldn't be able to find me. I could live my own life.

"What do you think, Mother?" I asked the small portrait of her that I'd had since before she died. In it she was looking at the viewer, smiling softly. The painter had obviously seen the lightness in her, and painted her in warm golds and oranges, the backdrop a soft blue, as if she were framed by a Midsummer sky. Looking at her portrait I was able to make believe she was listening, and loving me.

She had always been the kind one, softening Father's words with songs and stories. She had called me her darling boy, and kissed my hair. I'd thought the world of her.

I had inherited her flame-like red hair, and I sometimes wondered if I reminded Father of her, and that was why he was so harsh on me. Or perhaps he simply lost all his joy when she had passed.

Her sudden illness and then death had nearly killed me, too. It had certainly taken a lot of joy out of my life.

But I came out of mourning with a determination. I knew she would want me to continue living, and to make something of myself. I wanted to make her proud of me, as I knew she would be watching from Heaven.

I imagined her voice in my head.

All I want is for you to be happy, my boy, my darling Gideon. If this is your path, then you'd better take it. Live the best way you know how, and make me proud.

Her words seemed to come to me so clearly I felt I couldn't have simply imagined them, but perhaps Mother had sent the message down to me from beyond.

Full of sudden energy, I jumped up from the bed and dug out the old canvas bag I had from my time in the Navy and started filling it with my favourite things. My fine linen shirts and best breeches. But upon thinking it through, I'd have to dress down to get out of the house and to a ship.

What could I wear?

Could I take something off one of the gardeners? No, then they'd know that I was up to something.

I went to my wardrobe and pulled out my most ordinary white shirt and plain trousers and set them on my chair. I found the other few plain pieces of clothing I owned, then tucked in my favourite red coat as well. I simply couldn't leave it behind.

I finished packing my essentials, including a few of my favourite novels, the miniature portrait of my mother, and my comb and looking glass.

Before it became too late in the evening, I went down to dinner. It wouldn't do to make Father suspicious in any way.

I would leave in the morning, very, very early.

Far earlier than Father would be up, early enough to catch the ships leaving on the morning tides. Then I'd be gone, sailing away before he was even aware I wasn't in my bed.

I'd be safe, far away from him.

For now, I just had to pretend like everything was fine, and that I'd do as my father wished.

CHAPTER FOUR - IN WHICH A CAT FINDS GIDEON

*I*t was far too early to be awake. The sun hadn't even come up yet. In my room, I was pulling on my plainest trousers, plain white shirt and stuffing my feet into my most worn and sturdy boots.

The bag of my things sat packed and tied, ready next to my bedroom door.

The servants would probably be up already, but they'd be busy in the kitchen, and I should be able to sneak past them easily enough.

I took a last look at myself in the mirror. I'd tied my auburn hair back at the nape of my neck, and I hoped I'd pass for just an ordinary traveller looking for a berth on a ship.

Walking as softly as I could, I slipped out into the hallway, down the stairs and out the door. I had to hide behind the grandfather clock in the hallway when the scullery maid, Betsy, emerged from the back door and went into the kitchen. But once she was gone, I slipped out the door and escaped my father's house.

I quickly walked down the hill and to the wharves, and with

every step I felt a new sense of freedom and lightness.

No more Father, no more rules, no more wedding to a girl!

My mind exalted as I walked, and I found myself humming an old song from pure joy. The morning was misty, the fog clinging to the harbour and dripping up the hills. I heard the sounds of the sea as I got closer to the wharves - the cries of the fishermen, the creak of the ships and the general noise of morning business.

My next task started to loom in my mind, intimidating. I felt a little less joyful. I had a little money, but Father mostly controlled it all. I hoped I'd be able to find a ship willing to take me on... and that the ship wasn't full of bullies or otherwise cruel people.

How could I tell who I should go with? Then I thought of the man from the day before. That giant of a man with the teasing voice and sparkling eyes.

I walked the wharf slowly, not at all sure that the green painted ship - what had it been called? The Grey Kelpie? Would still be there.

Then I heard a familiar 'mrow' and there was a bump against my thigh. Zebulon the cat had found me again. I smiled and bent to scratch the ruff of fur at his neck and he looked up at me and seemed to smile back.

"Good morning," I said to him. "I guess that means your ship is still here. I don't suppose they take passengers, or are hiring for... not particularly skilled seamen?"

Zeb blinked his eyes very slowly, then he meowed once and started walking away. His tail straight up but tilted at the end just slightly.

I might as well follow and see if I can talk my way onto the ship, I thought. I did feel ridiculous following a cat through the busy morning wharves, but at least I had a semblance of a plan. Following a cat is better than aimless wandering, right?

Zeb led me back to the spot I'd fed him fish the day before.

"I don't have any fish," I said.

Zeb sat down and looked expectantly towards the ship where it was docked. I followed the direction of his gaze and saw someone coming down the gangplank and walking my way. He wasn't the man I'd met the day before, he wasn't as tall or as broad, and he wore all black: shirt, breeches and boots with a long black coat worn loose over the top. His hair was shaved at each side of his head but flowing and full on top, standing mostly up from his head in a fetching pompadour.

I watched him, torn between my desire to run - for he looked rather more dangerous than the man I'd met the day before - and to stay put, as it felt as if the cat had led me here precisely to meet him.

He looked at me, and then at the cat, and then back at me. His eyes were dark, flint shiny and about as hard.

"Zeb, what've you caught this time?" he asked. His voice matched his appearance, hard and gravelly. The kind of voice you dreaded hearing in an alleyway at night because it meant you were about to be robbed. Well, so I'd heard. Such a thing had never happened to me.

The cat didn't respond, just continued to gaze at the man expectantly.

The man in black flicked his eyes up to me. "Well? Who are you?"

"I'm ..." I stopped. I shouldn't just tell him my real name, should I? I was going to leave my life behind and that had to include a new name. "Aaron," I said. "I'm Aaron... Jones. I'm looking for a ship."

"You've found a ship," he said dryly. "You looking for work?"

I nodded. "Work, or I can pay for passage."

The man folded his arms and looked me up and down. I felt very skinny and useless. His shoulders may not have been as wide as the other man's but I could see from the thickness of his arms that he was well muscled. I spent most of my days walking or reading books.

"We don't take passengers," he said. "But we have been looking for a new cabin boy." He smirked then, and I felt my face flush.

Cabin boy? How humiliating. But it was probably the extent of what I could manage with my limited experience.

"Right," I said. "Um, what's the captain like?"

"Terrifying," he said. His face gave no expression. "But he'd probably like the look of you, especially if I tell him Zeb approved you. What experience have you had?"

"One year in the Royal Navy," I said.

"We'll try not to hold it against you," he said. "Come on, come aboard and we'll see if the Captain says yes."

With that he turned and headed back towards the ship. Zeb trotted along behind him, looking exceptionally pleased with himself.

"Um, you didn't give me your name," I said. I hurried to follow the cat and the man. "If you please?"

"If I please?" The man laughed, it wasn't a friendly laugh. "Call me Ezra."

"Ezra," I repeated back to myself. I made my way up the gangplank and onto the ship. *The vessel that would allow me to find my freedom*, I hoped.

Then I felt a sharp point prodding into my back. *Or maybe not?*

CHAPTER FIVE - IN WHICH GIDEON MEETS CAPTAIN TATE

"*W*ell, what have we here? The spy from yesterday?" Growled a somewhat familiar voice. The mountain of a man from yesterday. My heart beat rapidly in my chest, and I realised with cold dread that I had come from my father's house with no dagger, no sword, not a single thing to protect myself with.

What an idiot I am. Mother, if this is as far as I get, I hope you're not too disappointed.

"I'm not a spy," I managed to say. I dropped my bag on the deck of the ship and raised my arms so they could see I wasn't armed or really, any danger at all.

I looked over at Ezra, who was leaning against the mast, his arms folded. "This is Aaron," he said off handedly.

"Aaron. Why were you watching the ship yesterday?" The point of the blade withdrew from my back and I breathed a little easier. The man in the grey waistcoat moved in front of me. "And who are you?"

"I'm Aaron," I said. "Aaron Jones. I'm looking for a way off the island. Ezra said you might hire me on." I didn't want to say as what. I was sure I was already blushing and a ridiculous sight to see.

"Did he, now?" Grey Waistcoat said. "Or did he say that to you so that you'd come onto the ship and come face to face with pirates who could kidnap you and ransom you off?"

"Oh…" I said, faintly. I hadn't imagined they'd be pirates. Privateers or merchants, perhaps but… perhaps they knew who I was? My father would certainly pay a fine ransom to get me back. I'm his only heir after all.

How could I be so foolish?

The man in the grey waistcoat laughed loudly and sheathed his sword. "I'm just teasing you, lad. You can relax. We're not going to kidnap someone as ordinary as you. Have you got sea legs?"

"Yes, sir," I said. I lowered my hands, but I kept looking between the huge man and Ezra, uncertain if they were onto me or not. "One year in the Royal Navy."

"So you can read and write?"

"Yes, sir," I said again.

"Any languages other than English?"

"Latin and French."

"How old are you?"

"Twenty, sir."

"Wonderful." He nodded and looked me up and down, much as he had the day before, but in a slower, more lingering way that made me feel almost naked. He put a hand on his hip and nodded. "I'm in need of a factotum. We can't pay much, but if you want off the island, we sail in an hour on the morning tide."

I smiled. That's what I wanted, to leave. And within the hour!

But I couldn't forget the feel of the blade in my back. The man in the grey waistcoat, he was charming but frightening. If he wanted to throw me overboard he could probably do it with one hand. He could do all sorts of things to me, and I'd be powerless to resist. For some reason, rather than terrify me further, that thought made me feel warm all through.

I rubbed a hand over my eyes to try and hide the sudden excitement I felt, and nodded. "Yes, I would like to accept the terms of your offer," I said.

Grey Waistcoat and Ezra exchanged a look I couldn't decipher and then Grey Waistcoat shook my hand with a rough and strong grip. "Welcome aboard, lad. I'm Captain Tate. Ezra there is first mate, he'll show you around."

"Wonderful," Ezra said. He rolled his eyes. I was astounded at the lack of respect Ezra showed for his captain, but Tate just laughed again.

His laugh was full throated and hearty, it made me smile to hear it.

"And put him in the cabin behind mine," Tate said. "I'll want quick access to him when I have need."

My cheeks burned, thinking of alternate meanings to the Captain's words. Maybe Father had been right and I had been reading too many frivolous novels and ridiculous love stories.

Ezra sighed some and gestured with one hand. "Come along then, Aaron."

The ship wasn't the largest in dock, it was built for speed, but it was very well cared for. I could see that immediately.

The Captain may not insist on constant respect from his crew, but he ran a clean ship. It was a good sign, from my experience.

CHAPTER SIX - IN WHICH GIDEON FURNISHES HIS CABIN

The room Ezra showed me was indeed small, but it was private quarters. I had expected a hammock in a common room somewhere below decks. This was on the deck, directly behind the Captain's quarters.

The room held a narrow wooden slat bed with a cotton and down mattress on it, and a single blanket. There were hooks on the wall for hanging clothes, and a small table to one side. There were no decorations, but the walls were shining bright wood and the place felt very homely.

Something in me liked this room, which was so different to my rooms back home. I felt it boded well for my future, somehow.

"Thank you," I said to Ezra. I went inside and set my bag on the cot.

"Go to the quartermaster, she'll write you up on the papers and such, get it all above board, so to speak," Ezra said. "Captain will call when he needs you. You don't need to help with the sailing this time, he said."

"Thank you," I said again. I gave him a smile, genuinely grateful that I was leaving Jamaica, and in such a luxurious manner.

Ezra raised his eyebrows. For a moment I thought he would speak again, but he seemed to decide against it. He shook his head slightly and then left. I could hear the tap of his black boots recede up the deck.

I opened my bag and found the small, framed picture of my mother and set it in a small nook beside the pillow on my bed. There she could watch over me as I slept and I would feel safe - almost as if she were on the ship - or her spirit was guarding me like the angel I was sure she had become.

I dragged out the plain woollen overcoat I'd stuffed in at the last moment, hanging it on the hook closest to my door. I closed the door to see how the room felt with it shut and found it opened the room up a tiny bit. Made it feel more spacious.

There were hooks on the back of the door too, but I didn't want to pull out any of my finest clothing. I took my other, second plainest white shirt and hung it there.

Upon closer investigation there was a recessed shelf above the head of the bed. The kind with a rail along it, so I could put books in and they wouldn't fall out on my head in the middle of the night. I lovingly stowed my books in there, and then thought I'd better get to the quartermaster as soon as possible.

Had Ezra said 'she'?

Shaking my head, I opened the door to my room and found the way blocked quite effectively by Captain Tate.

"Hello, lad," he said.

I stared up at him, my breath catching in my throat. If he walked into the room he'd fill it. I'd have to hop up onto the bed and then... *I'd be in bed and he'd be filling the room...* I blushed again. My damn imagination, bringing up all those feelings and imaginings. It was ridiculously inappropriate.

As if he could read my mind, he winked at me. "Settling in all right?" He looked over my shoulder at the shelf of books. "Brought some reading matter, did you?"

He ducked his head and came into the room. I pressed myself back against the table, and consciously didn't get onto the bed. He was so close to me I could feel the heat of his body, hear his breath. My skin prickled with goosebumps.

"Yes, sir," I said, breathlessly.

"Call me Tate," he said. "I'm only Captain when it comes to hiring and if we're in a fight or a battle. The rest of the time, you can call me Tate."

"Tate," I echoed back. It felt completely wrong. I was going to call him Captain. He radiated power and command, but he was also strangely friendly and joking. I couldn't work him out, and that made me uncomfortable.

That and the things I kept imagining.

My mind went on another tangent, imagined him turning to me and kissing me deeply, pressing me back against the wall and... I shook my head. This was unbearable.

"Do you mind if I borrow this?" Tate picked up one of my paperbacks and turned to me. His arm brushed against my chest as he turned and I forgot how to breathe. He was looking at me again. I couldn't hold his gaze, I felt like he'd know what I'd just been imagining.

"Yes, of course," I said. "I should go and see the Quartermaster."

Without waiting for a response, I slipped out of the room. I couldn't help brushing against him as I left - the room was so small.

Out on the deck I took a deep breath of fresh air and hurried to the back of the ship.

CHAPTER SEVEN - IN WHICH GIDEON MAKES A FRIEND OR TWO

I made quite a mess of introducing myself to the Quartermaster, because I was confused at what I was seeing.

"Quartermaster?" I called, knocking on the door to the cabin.

"Come on in, Sugar," a voice called out, husky and sweet.

I pushed the door open and went in. Inside was an Indian woman in a loose white shirt, a long wide skirt and a fitted brown waistcoat covered in pockets. There was a thick belt around her waist with a few pouches and pockets and a sheathed dagger hanging off it.

Only she wasn't a woman of the kind I'd ever seen before.

Her face was absolutely gorgeous, she had high cheekbones and a firm jaw. Her jaw was covered in a close cropped black beard, only a quarter inch long. Her eyes were large and lined heavily with kohl, making them look brighter and even more alluring.

"Hello?" I said.

"Hello?" She said back. "I'm Sagorika, the Quartermaster. You must be the new cabin boy."

"Yes, Gid-" I choked on my real name. I coughed to try and cover up the slip of my tongue and cleared my throat before continuing. "Aaron. Jones."

Sagorika gave me a knowing smile. "Well, Aaron, let me tell you something right away. This ship isn't like any you've sailed with before."

"I know," I said. Then realised it could sound rude, though I hadn't meant it that way, I'd just noticed so much oddness already. "I mean, please excuse me, but I have noticed some strangeness."

Sagorika wasn't insulted though, she laughed a throaty laugh and wiggled her fingers at me. "I'm sure you have questions, ask me anything you need to know." She turned and pulled down a huge ledger book from a high railed shelf.

"Uh, the captain?" I managed to say. I was sure so unsure of where to start, or how to phrase what I wanted to know. I don't even know if I knew what I wanted to know, and that was making my head spin.

Sagorika paused to look at me, her smile soft and her head tilted to one side. "That's all you want to ask about? Well, Tate runs the ship as a democracy," Sagorika said. "Everyone gets an equal share and an equal say - unless we're in a battle or a raid."

"Does... does that happen often?" I asked.

"We'll see," she said lightly. She opened the ledger and wrote Aaron Jones down on a list of crew, then handed me the pen. "Sign next to your name, please."

I took the pen and had to consciously write 'Aaron Jones' instead of Gideon Keene. I was so aware of her watching me, and my hand hesitating over the words.

"What other questions do you have, love?" Sagorika asked.

I swallowed. "Um, I don't think I have any," I said.

"Well, let me tell you something anyway. You've obviously had a look at me. I don't have to hide who I am on this ship, and that's true for the whole crew. It's a place where no one is judged or made fun of for living their true self, whatever it may be."

That sounded far too good to be true. It was one thing to want to wear a dress, but it was quite another to have fantasies about kissing men. I would have to continue to hide that part of myself, probably forever. But at least I wasn't being forced to marry a woman on this ship.

The silence stretched out, and I realised Sagorika expected me to respond in some way. "Thank you," I said. It felt silly, weak, not nearly enough. "I'm... I'm confident that I'm going to enjoy being onboard, I think."

"You will, honey. Now you have a place to sleep?"

"Yes, ma'am I do, behind the Captain's quarters."

"Good. We're all done here for now, so go watch the waves or something until the Captain starts in on jobs you could be doing."

I thanked her and went back out on the deck. The crew were casting off, shouts going back and forth from the ship and the dock.

I felt tears welling up in my eyes and quickly blinked, trying to stop them from spilling out.

How little would they all think of me if they saw me crying?

I looked at Kingston, my eyes wandering up the hill, past the market, past the houses of the middle classes and up to the Governor's house. My Father's house. The sun had been up less than half an hour and the sunlight caught on the windows. It was too far away to see which window was mine, or any details about it at all, but I imagined my father waking up. He was slow to wake in the mornings. It would be another hour at least before anyone missed me.

And what would he say when I was discovered missing? He'd probably assume I had gone to the market and would turn up later in the day. Maybe they wouldn't miss me until dinner time, or later.

My stomach rumbled, empty and aching at the same time. My father could demand a lot of me, but also he wouldn't miss me for most or possibly all of a day. How strange to live in such an in between space in his affections.

I felt alone in the world, which had, of course, caused the entire plan. But I had only expected exhilaration, not this bereft stomach ache.

"Ro-orwl." I looked down to see Zeb the cat rubbing himself against my leg. I smiled down at him, despite myself. I bent down to scratch between his ears. He meowed at me prettily and I chuckled.

"Thanks for getting me aboard," I said.

"You're welcome," a dry voice behind me said. I startled, leaping in mid air to face the voice. Zeb yowled angrily and ran away across the deck, his claws skittering over the wooden planks.

Ezra watched me, one eyebrow raised and an unimpressed grimace on his face. My heart raced and I tried to gather myself together, but my dignity was long gone.

"Of course, thank you, Ezra," I said quickly.

"Are you even interested in where we going?"

I shook my head looking back towards Kingston. "No, it really doesn't matter as long as I'm not here. I don't mind where we sail to."

Ezra looked at me, one eyebrow arching and a smile tugging at the corner of his mouth, which was a little less unimpressed and a little more warm.

"Really? What happened to you back there? It must have been terrible."

I considered how to answer him. If I were being honest I would tell him nothing happened to me here and that's part of the problem. But I wasn't being myself, I had to be Aaron and Aaron had to have a good reason to leave and not care where he went. My mind raced as I tried to think of something feasible.

"I got in with somebody - somebody bad for me," I said. I had a flash of brilliance. I stole the backstory of the hero from one of my favourite romance stories. "I was set up, uh, framed for something I didn't do."

"I guess that kind of thing happens a lot in Kingston." Ezra seemed amused now. I wondered if he could see through my lies, and didn't believe me. I wasn't exactly used to lying - with the exception of lying to my father, perhaps. I tried to think of some details that would make the story sound more authentic.

"Yes, we were playing... cards," I said. "I was winning. They said I cheated. I didn't cheat but I couldn't prove I hadn't. And uh, they hid a card on me, there was a lot of money at stake of course, because we were gambling, and things got out of hand."

Ezra looked even more amused. "Yes, I can see how that would be a problem. People don't like to be cheated at cards. We'll get you far away from all of that."

There was a lightness to his voice. Suddenly the grumpy growly timbre to his voice had eased and he sounded a lot more friendly.

I wondered how much he could see through me and if he was going to tell the others. I felt sure my face was flushed, giving me away. Something about the way he looked at me made me feel exposed, as if he could read my thoughts.

"It's funny," he continued, moving a little closer to me. "Watching you there, looking at the view. It's as if you're sad to leave, not glad for the escape."

I turned to look at Kingston once more and wrapped my arms around myself without thinking. Then I realised I was doing it and immediately dropped my arms down.

"I guess I am sad," I said. I had to cover for my atrocious lying. "This strange little port town has been my home for a long time." I hoped using that language would make me seem worldly.

"I see."

The ship's sails filled with wind and the ship pulled away from the docks. I braced a hand on the railing as the deck moved.

This is it. I was really leaving my old life behind. I felt tears welling in my eyes again and swallowed trying to keep it in.

Ezra was still right there and what would he think if he saw me crying?

I wanted to impress him. He was so impressive himself.

The ship started to move, rolling up and down with the waves and I could feel the wind as we picked up speed. This boat handled a lot nicer than the naval ship that I had been on before.

I looked up at the masts and wondered if they would try to make me climb them.

As I stared upwards, my confusion over my conflicted feelings of leaving Kingston crashed against my past and a memory came to me unbidden but as powerful as a punch to the stomach.

I cling to the mast as a storm rolls up. My shipmates call for me to come down. The captain calls for me to secure the rigging, and me - frozen - unable to move. My knuckles are white, clinging to the wood. The fear I felt paralysing me. Watching in terror as the grey clouds close in, the waves starting to get higher, the spray soaking me. Then the rain and the terrible moment when the thunder starts and still I am there up in the rigging unable to move for fear I'll slip and dash my head on the deck below.

"Are you alright?" Ezra closed his hand around my shoulder surprisingly tender and comforting again. I startled, brought back to the present.

I had embarrassed myself once more. I looked into his eyes, humiliated to realise that my face was damp from tears. I quickly swiped my hand and then my sleeve over my face and cleared my throat. "Yes, I'm fine."

"It's only, you've gone whiter than my grandmother's wedding sheets." Ezra looked concerned rather than amused despite the joke he'd made. "Also you're crying."

"Oh, yes, I am," I said. I rubbed my face again with my sleeve. "I just had a bad memory."

"From Jamaica? Or the Navy perhaps?"

I nodded. "It's nothing, don't concern yourself about it."

"I can't help but feel responsible, and a little concerned. I got you on the ship, after all. If you're going to be a lunatic it'll be my fault and the captain wouldn't like that."

"It's nothing like that." That felt like the biggest lie of them all because if I did have to climb the mast again I don't know what I'd do and even the thought of it made my heart race again.

Plus, unbidden, I imagined Father's face when he realised I'd gone. I didn't feel sorry for him exactly but something like it. Even though in a lot of ways I hated and feared him, he was still my father and I loved him too. It sickened me to imagine that I'd hurt him.

I tried to banish the thoughts out of my mind and focus on Ezra instead.

Up close like this, I could see how handsome he was, not in the same way as the Captain was handsome. Ezra had dangerous devil-may-care aspects to him, rather than the raw, untamed attractiveness of the Captain.

For a moment I imagined reaching up and touching his chest then sliding down my hand down to feel the hardness of his waist. The muscles there must be taut as the mainsheet. Thinking about his body, I know I blushed again.

His hand was still on my shoulder and I realised he was rubbing his thumb against my shirt - or my shoulder, rather - in a comforting manner. I could smell seaspray and the distant smoke of Kingston but also Ezra's musky scent, and it was doing things to me. Pleasant things certainly, but unwelcome ones. I pulled back abruptly.

"It's nothing," I said again.

Ezra eyes never left mine and I found it almost impossible to break away. I couldn't look down. It felt as if he saw right through to my soul, and my soul saw his in return.

My heart lurched. I felt locked to him, as if we were fated to meet, and then do something epic.

"You're a strange one, Aaron," Ezra said. "Just remember though, that almost all of us on this ship are running from something."

"I beg your pardon?" I asked, my voice low.

"The Captain, myself, all of us. In fact, my even being in this harbour was astoundingly reckless, and yet, I wandered the streets as if it were nothing. It is up to all of us to make peace with what we've done and live as best we can."

I opened my mouth to ask him what he meant, but he turned away. I felt released from his gaze as if the thing connecting us had severed. I fancied it as a shimmering chain that had held us together but was now broken.

It was a relief as well as a loss. I took a moment to catch my breath - I hadn't even realised I had been holding it - and turned back to see the isle of Jamaica fading as we sailed away.

My breath hitched in my chest - whether from watching my home vanish or from what had passed between Ezra and I, I couldn't say.

I could hear Ezra walking away and I wondered if he had felt the same connection I had. Was the strange soul chain as real for him as it had been for me? If it had been, he was doing well at hiding it.

Probably it was all in my imagination.

How was I ever going to survive this voyage?

CHAPTER EIGHT - IN WHICH GIDEON TALKS TO A CAT

The crew ate well that night on fresh meat and vegetables from the port town.

"Don't get used to this sort of thing," Captain Tate said. He nudged me with his elbow and I had to fight to stay upright from the force of it. "Soon enough we'll be back on salted meat and hard tack. Oh, and fish. I hope you like fish."

"It's fine with me," I said.

The crew sniggered at my response, and I flushed.

"Well, that's lucky," Captain Tate said, amused.

Shouldn't have made it sound like he needed my permission. Or that I was discussing the menu plan for a fine party at the Governor's house...

My cheeks burned, so I picked up my cup and drank, hoping it would cool me down. The spiced rum in the cup did the opposite and the hairs at the back of my neck prickled, hearing the crew continuing to laugh. I would rather none of them paid any attention to me at all but I suppose being the new person on deck meant I was a novelty, exotic. Surely, it would pass in time.

Captain Tate told me I had no duties until the next day. He

suggested that I take the time to settle in, and I resolved to have an early night.

I went to my cabin and started to get ready for bed. I had been up an awfully long time that day, after all.

I was washing my face in the basin when a strange noise nudged at my awareness. A soft scratch at the door? I opened it to find Zeb the cat looking up at me with his huge green eyes.

He meowed at me once, then promptly pushed past my legs and jumped up on my bed.

"Don't get too comfortable there," I said. He'd situated himself in the centre of the bed with no room for me, and I had the idea he'd be very difficult to move once he was settled. He looked at me and then started washing his leg.

Sighing, I shut the door, extinguished the lantern and got into bed. Zeb had many long complaints about me getting under the blankets and we had to negotiate who got which part of the bed, how much of the blanket.

Then once I was fully laid down he promptly climbed onto my lap.

"Thanks for keeping me warm," I said. The cat was doing a sort of two-step dance, his paws kneading up and down on my legs. The low rumble of his purr seemed to fill the room. His little furry face seemed to smile at me and he blinked his eyes slowly as he sat, tucking his paws under his chest and gazing into my face.

"Well, at least someone is happy that I'm here," I said. Zeb looked incredibly pleased with himself.

"My father never let me have a pet before," I said, because now that I was talking to a cat out loud, I may as well continue. Besides, it made the whole evening seem less lonely. "Are you smart? I used to want a puppy. It would play fetch and be my friend all the time. I never really had friends either." I sighed, the cat continued to gaze at me and I began to feel like he understood what I was saying.

Well, as I spoke his nose twitched, it was a little like understanding. "But a cat would have been lovely too. Someone to talk to, at the very least." The cat blinked again. "I rather think you understand me." I reached my hand out to scratch between his ears. The purring got louder and his eyes glittered with pleasure. "You're not an ordinary cat are you? Will you be my friend?"

I probably should have felt silly talking to a cat like that, but it really did feel like he could be unusual, extraordinary. So, I told him my secrets. "I'm not an ordinary boy either. I don't want to date or marry a woman. I think that they are pretty and all, but I've never wanted to kiss one. I want to kiss a man and that can only mean scandal and impropriety. So, I ran away from home and here I am on the ship with some very strange men I keep having horribly good - no, very bad and dirty thoughts about."

Zeb blinked at me.

"Yeah, he's really, really very attractive. Like, those eyes and how he smiles," I continued.

Zeb didn't respond aside from closing his eyes and going to sleep.

"I can see that I'm boring you," I said, extinguishing the lamp and settling into the bed.

It felt liberating to say all that out loud, even if it was just to a cat who didn't care what I said.

CHAPTER NINE - IN WHICH GIDEON
LEARNS SOMETHING NEW

The next morning, I woke with a crushing pressure on
my chest and something fluffy beating at my face. I
woke with a start, struggling to draw a breath.

Zeb sat on my chest and was hitting my face with one paw.

"Aah! What? What is it?" I cried.

The cat peered into my eyes and then half turned to look
meaningfully at the door. The door was closed fast, and the cat
couldn't get out.

"Right," I said. "But you're going to have to get off me if you
want me to get up and open the door."

Zeb eyed me distrustfully but then nimbly jumped down
onto the floor and sauntered to the door. I disentangled my legs
from the bedding and hurried over to open the door for him. He
slipped out.

"Not so much as a thank you, eh?" I called after him,
somewhat miffed at my rude awakening.

"What was that?"

A chill went down my back and I turned to see the Captain
approaching. He was dressed and groomed, very handsome

indeed although he still looked like he could tear an arm off me if he tried. The size of those biceps.

I swallowed. I hoped he hadn't thought I was being rude to him?

"Uh, nothing, Captain," I said. "Just talking to the cat. I'll dress and be right out."

"Take your time," he said, genially. "Oh, and remember. You should call me Tate, not Captain."

I slammed the door shut before he could see inside, aware I was in only my nightclothes, which felt somehow like I was totally naked.

That morning I shadowed Captain Tate around the ship, learning about the stores of food and the way pay was divvied up amongst the crew and generally where things were so that I could do my job.

"Although, I suspect we won't be keeping you terribly busy with work," Tate said.

We were in his quarters, and I had realised as soon as I entered the room that his bed must be directly on the other side of the wall to mine. Although I was sure there'd have been no way he could have overheard what I'd said the night before, I was hot with shame over it. One night of freedom and I had utterly lost my head.

I absolutely have to be more careful about what I say and when I say it.

Bent over the desk, he was showing me his log and what information should be entered in each day.

It wasn't a large room, and the captain was so tall and broad, and the desk so small that it made sense to press in against him to read the log. At first I had tried not to, but there really was no way to see what he was talking about unless I was right there beside him.

The heat of his body alongside mine was unmistakable, I couldn't ignore it, although I did desperately try.

Think of unsexual things. Playing cricket on the lawn. The girls in their frocks at Father's parties. Father. Collecting butterflies in jars to study their wings. Birdwatching. The grey wings of the gulls almost the colour of the vest Captain Tate is wearing today.

Captain Tate is right there.

He smells like smoke and danger.

"Are you all right, Aaron?" Captain Tate's voice was a low rumble beside me.

"Yes, quite," I said. My voice came out breathy and strained.

"Is there anything I can do to help... relax you?"

I quickly turned to look into his face. He was smiling again, his eyes sparkling with a beautifully tempting invitation.

"No." I pulled back from the desk and away from him, crashing into the chair behind me, which I struggled to right.

Captain Tate's hand closed over mine where it rested on the top of the chair. "Aaron, you're trembling," he said, his voice very soft. "And I think I know why."

"No, no I'm not," I said. Although I don't know if he believed me, his hand was over mine after all. He could feel the trembling that was washing over my entire body. He could probably hear the pounding of my heart, because it was drowning out the sounds of the sea in my own ears.

"You are," he said gently. "Are you afraid of me?"

"Of course not, Captain," I said. "I'm merely... merely..." I trailed off, uncertain of what I was about to say. Captain Tate leaned in, his expression softening.

"I'd like to kiss you, Aaron," he rumbled, hardly loud enough to hear.

"I... what?" I gasped. Reflexively, I went to move away from him but his arm slipped around my body, there was a soft pressure there, guiding me towards him, but with enough slack that were I to pull away I could. If I really tried.

I stood frozen.

He couldn't possibly have said what I thought he said, could he? He wants to kiss me? I must be hallucinating. One day at sea and I've lost my wits entirely.

"I'm sorry, I don't think I heard you correctly."

"I heard you pretty clearly last night," he said. His eyes sparkled a little and his smile became positively cheeky.

My entire body stiffened - *he'd heard me.*

"You don't like girls, you like men. *And* you think I'm attractive," Captain Tate said. "Well, I think you're the most beautiful boy I've ever seen, so refined, so uncertain. I would like to kiss you, if you would let me."

My mouth was completely dry and my face was hot.

He leaned in closer still.

Can this be? Is this a dream? Did I make my fantasy into reality simply by speaking it out loud? But it's so improper, in so many ways, how could I possibly?

"But sir, I'm your factotum," I said, weakly.

Tate's face broke into a wide toothy grin. "Is that your only objection?"

"I've never done anything like this before, I..." I swallowed hard.

What am I afraid of? If he is suggesting it, he will not throw me off the ship for my predilections. He wants me, he thinks I'm beautiful and refined.

And I most definitely want him.

"Let me show you how it's done, then," he said. Leaning in, he pressed his mouth to mine so gently and so sweetly I thought I might very well pass out right there.

It was as if the world fell into place for me. Something that had always been off centre, or just not fitting correctly into the puzzle of my life slid into place.

My head filled with air and sunshine and for once the worried voice inside my head went quiet.

My body knew what to do. I didn't think about it, but in an instant my arms were around his neck, pulling him down to me and kissing him back with a ferocity I had no idea I was capable of. I was making noises, strangely high, needful noises.

Tate responded by partially lifting me, one arm wrapping tight around my waist and half carrying me to the bed.

I made another sound I wasn't aware I could make. A kind of low groan in the back of my throat and he laid me back on his bed, kissing me again and again.

Good lord but this is the best thing that's ever happened to me, I thought.

"Do you want this?" he asked, and his breath was quick and his gaze intense. I tingled all over, anticipation and desire throwing all my concern and propriety out the door and overboard.

I nodded, although I hardly knew what I was agreeing to, I simply knew I wanted it. "Please," I gasped. "I've never, before... I don't know what to do."

He smiled and leaned close to kiss me again, softly, demanding nothing. His hands moved over my chest and he undid the buttons on my shirt, pulling it open and smoothing his rough fingers over my skin.

I broke the kiss to watch him explore me, the stark contrast of his tanned and rough hands against the pale smoothness of my chest.

He removed my clothes with surprising gentleness and then straightened up to undress himself. I felt exposed, vulnerable below him, but I wasn't afraid.

He opened his pants and shoved them down his hips, revealing a great mass of black hair and a heavy, long cock.

My mouth went dry and I shuddered bodily. *I wanted it.*

"You've never done this before, so it's probably easier if I bottom," he said, his voice low.

"Bottom?" I asked.

He reached to stroke my cock with one hand and I melted into the bed, moaning like I imagined one of the doxies back home did several times a night. Tate smiled in response and slipped his other hand under my waist, pulling me up the bed and then rolling over so he was laid on the mattress and I was balanced on top of his body.

So much of my skin was touching so much of his, he was warm and hard beneath me. His pubic hair trailed up his stomach towards his naval and I had the urge to put my head down and lick at the skin either side. I wanted to, but I wasn't sure if that would be a good idea or simply bizarre. I braced my hands on his biceps and didn't move, uncertain.

"Don't be afraid," he said. "You won't hurt me." I imagined he could've easily said those words in a way that was mocking, but there was no mirth in his tone. He was reassuring me.

I nodded and shifted, dragging my hips up against his so that our cocks rubbed together. I nearly lost my control in that instant, the feeling was so divine, teasing myself and him in the same moment.

This had an incredible effect on Captain Tate. He groaned louder than I had, and I felt his body under mine moving like the sea itself, surging up against me, buoying me up. Emboldened by the effect I was having on him, I dragged my hips down again, this time moaning with him as I felt my body shudder, pleasure shooting through every inch of me. I could feel my cock dripping with pleasure.

"Oh, you're a fucking little tease, are you?" His voice was a low growl which sent another few drops spilling out of me. Tate's hand pressed into the small of my back, forcing more pressure between us. I shuddered, sure I was about to reach fulfilment at any moment. He seemed to sense this and his hand moved between us instead.

"Sit up," he ordered and I did so without question.

I straddled his wide thighs, my own legs spreading apart by necessity to allow the movement. Tate pushed himself up on one elbow and looked at me, his mouth falling open.

"My god, you're so gorgeous," he said. "What I wouldn't give to have you ride me..." He swallowed and shook his head.

"I..." I wanted that too, the thought of him filling me with that magnificent cock was heavenly, but also somewhat frightening. Something in me wanted very much to please him, but at the same time I hesitated. He sat all the way up, slipped an arm around me and kissed my neck. The feel of his lips and the brush of his beard there sent another shiver of pleasure through me.

"Next time." He growled and I whimpered, pressing myself against his chest with longing for something I couldn't begin to articulate. I slipped my arms around him and took comfort in the warmth of his skin.

Would there be a next time? I could hardly dare to hope...

He reached an arm out, and curious, I rested my cheek on his shoulder to watch. He picked up a small pot from the side of his bed and opened it one handed. He dipped a finger inside and it came out coated with something clear and gooey.

"Coconut oil," he said.

He reached below us, I could feel his wrist against me, but he was doing something to himself. With a grunt he lay back, letting go of me. Even more curious, I shifted back and between his legs as he hitched them up. I wanted to watch this. If - as he had promised - there was a next time, I wanted to learn everything I could.

It was the most salacious thing I had ever witnessed. With two deft fingers he stretched his own ass open. As he did his breath hitched and he moaned softly. Tearing my eyes away from this incredible sight, I looked up at his face. He was biting his lip, his eyebrows pulled together and his entire expression seemed to scream bliss.

I panted, my hand moving to pump my own cock without my mind considering if it was a good idea.

Seeing this, he reached for me with his free hand and drew me closer in as he slowly withdrew his fingers from inside himself.

"Inside me," he whispered, his voice heavy with hunger.

I pressed my hips close against his thighs, and slowly pressed myself inside him. He guided me with his hand on my hip, and underneath me - the power of him - willingly surrendered.

Breathless again, I reached a hand up to stroke his chest, my hips pressing forward and forward until I was fully sheathed inside him.

My heart hammered in my chest, I was panting hard, and

every part of me sought to release the pressure. Tate closed his eyes and I leaned forward to kiss his mouth, wanting reassurance that he was there in that moment with me.

He opened his eyes and smiled into the kiss.

"Aaron, you fit perfectly," he said. I winced a little. In this, most intimate of moments, he made me feel a fraud. My made up name shouldn't be what he was saying to me in this moment.

But how could I tell him the truth now? While this was happening?

"What is it, what's wrong?" He asked. I swallowed. I really should get better at hiding my emotions, but here with him, with me inside of him, I couldn't keep up a pretence.

"Call me Gideon?" I asked, my voice soft.

"Gideon," he repeated. "Oh-Of course." I could see the question in his eyes but he didn't pursue it. "Rock your hips and fuck me, Gideon."

Although I'm sure my colour was already high, I could feel my cheeks burn with the coarseness of the language he used. I moved my hands down his chest, lingering on his nipples and then the hard muscles in his midsection before gripping his hips. I pushed inside, pulled most of the way out and pushed in again, groaning as waves of pleasure flooded every fibre of my being.

His mouth moved down my jaw and to the soft skin of my throat where he kissed and then sucked. The sting of pain as he sucked harder at first made me hiss, but then the pain melted into an intense warmth and I felt a shiver rack through me.

I couldn't speak any longer, lost entirely to the physical sensations of loving him with my body. The glide and pull, the delicious tease of what was waiting just beyond.

His hand - still slick with oil - slipped down to fist around his cock and pumped, and a flash of jealous possession took me.

I slapped his hand away and closed my fist on him instead. He was mine to enjoy now, and I would be responsible for his pleasure.

I heard him moan as I wrapped my fingers around the vein-laced shaft and pumped it. This I knew how to do.

How many nights had I spent doing this to myself, imagining myself in a situation just like this? I pumped my hand slowly, playing him in counterpoint to the surging of my hips against him.

Tate's hands moved up my arms, caressing me and teasing at my skin. His fingers stroked down my neck and I moaned, feeling myself reaching the crest of pleasure.

I tightened my hold on his cock and stroked it with long movements, the kind which would always get me to completion in little time. My hips sped to a frenzy, thrusting into him with a frantic need.

My eyes fixed on Tate's face, he was watching me with wide, gorgeous eyes - his need clear. I stroked him once more and felt his pulsing in my hand, followed swiftly by the wetness of his ejaculate.

I climaxed inside him almost in the same instant, as his body clenched around me, squeezing my cock in the most delicious and satisfying way. I heard myself cry out - a sound of pleasure and triumph.

I collapsed forward onto him, panting as if I'd run the length of Jamaica. His chest was moving rapidly up and down under my cheek and his hand stroked my back with a stuttering movement.

CHAPTER TEN - IN WHICH GIDEON LEARNS SOMETHING ELSE

"Well, that was a surprise," he said, after a few minutes of us both trying to catch our breath.

"Y-yes," I said. My head was clearing and I began to feel suddenly afraid.

I had asked him to call me Gideon. Surely he would ask about my name and demand the truth? I chewed on my lower lip, which felt tender and swollen from all the kissing, and waited for the proverbial axe to drop.

Instead he just petted my back, in much the same way I had petted Zeb the night before.

Now soft, I pulled myself out of him and shifted further up his chest, tucking my cheek against his shoulder.

"Did you enjoy it, Gideon?"

I closed my eyes and smiled. "Yes." In truth, I had loved it, and wanted nothing more than to try it again, be less clumsy and more focused on Tate's needs, but I was still afraid.

"Good, so did I," he murmured. His hand stroked up my spine and into my hair, tangling his fingers in the auburn strands and pulling gently. That felt amazing too. "So, shall we talk about the name thing?"

I tensed instantly. His hand stroked my hair again and then down my back. I wanted to be comforted by it, and I was on some level, but I wasn't at all sure what he was going to say to me.

"I - I uh," I said.

"Let me tell you a story," he said. "Many years ago, when I was younger, I didn't used to be the captain of a pirate ship, I used to be a merchant. And I had a partner - Solomon - he wasn't just my business partner, but my partner in bed as well."

I sat up, staring into his face. "Did you just say pirate ship?" My voice was choked with fear.

Captain Tate sat up as well. "Yes? You didn't realise?"

"I - I, uh, I - " I cleared my throat, my head spinning. I shrank back from the Captain and my back crashed into the wood of the wall behind me.

I joined a pirate ship?

"It's nothing for you to worry about," Tate said. "Really, I thought you knew."

I swallowed. It felt like the ocean under me was surging.

I lost my virginity to a pirate captain. I ran away from home and jumped onto a pirate ship? I am in so much trouble. I'm going to die. Father's ships are probably hunting this one as I sit here. I'm likely to be blasted to Kingdom Come just for being on board, and Father would never even know.

What have I done?

Tate reached out to touch my hand but I flinched back, out of his reach. "Aaron? Gideon? What - whatever your name is, you don't have to be afraid. I'm here for you, and you're safe on this ship."

I didn't mean to, but I pulled my hand back from his touch. It was all too much to take in. I was afraid, and I felt naked - I *was* naked - and exposed.

"I'm sorry, I need to think this through," I said. I scrambled out of his bed, cast around for my clothes and got dressed as fast as I could.

"Stay, let us talk," Tate said. I paused, pulling my trousers up and gazed at him. His eyebrows were drawn together, his eyes wide. Nothing like the contented expression he had held moments earlier.

"I - I can't," I said. "I'm sorry."

I pulled my shirt on and fled the room without looking at him again.

What have I gotten myself into? And how can I possibly get out of it?

The problem, I discovered, with ships, is that they're actually very small. If you're trying to avoid someone on a ship, it's nearly impossible. Especially when that person is the Captain of said ship.

And he's roughly eight feet tall and five feet across.

In addition, you are employed to be his factotum.

All of these things made avoiding Tate and getting time to think almost impossible.

He was on the deck, so I went to my cabin. But then I thought that it was exceedingly easy to find me in my cabin, so I went below decks to the galley, but there were crew sleeping in hammocks in the hallway to the galley, and in the galley was Cook.

I tried heading aft to see if there were any quiet spaces at all.

I went down another ladder, past the food stores and went towards the stern of the ship.

There I found what must be the brig, although I found it hard to imagine Captain Tate keeping anyone in the brig for any length of time. He appeared to be quite soft hearted, despite how terrifying he looked.

No, he's a pirate, he might just be as terrifying as I first thought. You couldn't be a pirate and not be comfortable with killing people. Stealing. Sinking ships full of innocent souls.

I sat down on the bench outside the brig's bars and rested my head in my hands.

"What have I done?" I moaned to myself.

I've lost my virginity to a pirate is what I've done. And now I'm trapped on a ship with him. And he's beautiful and terrifying and I am most certainly going to die.

The thoughts spiralled in my head and I forgot how to breathe.

My hands clawed at my hairline, and I stared at the floor in between my feet. My most boring boots. I was going to die in my least interesting and flattering outfit.

Of all the things to worry about, at a time like this.

I barked out a laugh.

Pathetic. I'm completely pathetic. I could well have taken my life in my hands even by running out on the Captain, because pirate captains could be wilful and proud and maybe I insulted him, and now I'm worried about my wardrobe?

I don't know how long I sat there, head in my hands, looking between my feet at the wooden boards. My thoughts continued to spiral - *I lost my virginity to a pirate and now I'm going to die.*

Until finally, I wore myself out, curled up on my side on the bench and fell asleep.

CHAPTER ELEVEN - IN WHICH GIDEON SHOWS EZRA MORE THAN HE MEANS TO

I startled awake when someone touched my shoulder.

"Aaron? What're you doing down here?"

I flinched back from the touch. Ezra's voice. Ezra had found me.

"I'm fine," I said.

I felt disgusting, my clothes were sweaty and dirty, my trousers stuck to me in particularly unpleasant ways and my hair fell lank and greasy around my face. Besides, my shoulder and hip were aching from leaning against the hard wooden bench.

"What are you doing down here?"

I stood up, Ezra had to move backwards because he was standing so close. I cleared my throat, and tried to adjust my trousers without looking like I was, but again, he was right there. He noticed.

"Are you all right?"

I shook my head. "Not... Not exactly." My hair had fallen loose, I gathered it in one hand and pulled it into a twist at the back of my neck.

Ezra's eyes caught on something below my chin and his eyes widened. "What is that?" He asked.

"What is what?" I felt suddenly terrified that he would know what the captain and I had done. He couldn't *tell* could he? No, there was no chance. Was there?

"Captain said not to bother about finding you, which I thought was odd in the first place," Ezra said. His voice had dropped considerably and now was a barely audible rumble. "But now, here you are, hiding in the stern of the ship with a great, big, stinking love bite on your neck." He prodded my neck and I winced, it hurt more than it should have.

Like I had a bruise there.

In the exact place Tate had bitten and sucked at me. He'd left a mark? I didn't even know that was a thing that could happen...

My hand flew up to cover the sensitive area. "I, I uh, don't know what you mean," I said.

Ezra frowned and folded his arms. I tried to move back to give him room as he seemed to be taking up more and more space.

It was like I could taste the rage wafting off him. Or like it was vibrating the floorboards of the ship.

"A love bite. The Captain. You're hiding. You two fucked, didn't you?"

I felt my entire head going scarlet. He *could* tell! And he seemed angry about it.

"I cannot -" I gasped. "I cannot have this conversation."

"You did, don't deny it. It all adds up." He leaned in towards me and sniffed. "Well. I don't care, anyway. You do whatever you like."

"Wait," I wanted to stop him. His thunderous countenance made my stomach churn as if I would be sick. I hated to see people angry because of me. "It's not, it's not what it looks like. I don't - I don't intend to do anything of the sort again, he's a -" I bit my lip. I couldn't continue. I was about to say because he's a filthy pirate, but of course Ezra would be one too.

"He's a what?" Ezra growled. He leaned in closer to me, crowding me back against the bench and the wall behind it. I felt my breath get shallow and quick. There was no arguing with him. I was sure if I denied him information he would just keep leaning in on me, and that was simultaneously terrifying and exciting.

My traitorous body was reacting to his proximity and it was telling me that Ezra was big and powerful and sensual and that I wanted to be naked with him and bite his lip and... I shook my head. Anything was better than being plagued by these thoughts.

I may as well tell him the truth. Maybe it'll make him back off and I won't be tormented by desire quite so much.

"I won't do it again because he's a pirate," I whispered.

Ezra peered into my eyes, his expression inscrutable.

"Yes. A pirate," he said. Then he turned and left the room, the heels of his boots ringing against the floorboards. How had I not heard him approach before?

I was asleep. I must've been very deeply asleep after my ... exertions.

For a moment I stayed against the wall, my chest heaving as I tried to steady my breath.

What should I do now?

There was nothing for it. I had to follow him. I couldn't hide below decks forever. In the long term, I had to get off the ship. That meant staying aboard until the next port, wherever that was.

I followed Ezra, but I gave him a long head start. I didn't want it to look like we had been spending time together down there. If the crew of the ship knew about Captain Tate and his predilections... and surely someone would have seen me leave his cabin in a hurry. Maybe people already suspected, in which case I didn't want them thinking I'd immediately run off and done the same thing with the First Mate.

I emerged onto the deck, blinking in the bright sunlight and ran right into Captain Tate - my nose collided with his chest.

I flinched back from him and he gripped me by one shoulder, steadying me. I startled some and he quickly removed his hand.

"Aaron, Gideon, are you all right? I've been worried..."

"I - I, uh," had I been all right?

No.

Obviously not.

But propriety held me back from a frank and honest answer. Even though I knew now that the ship wasn't a common merchantman or shipping vessel, he was still the ship's Captain.

More to the point, I was in his employ.

I must be polite, and bland and make no trouble for him.

"I'm quite alright," I said, faintly.

Captain Tate peered at my face and tilted his head to one side. "Are you sure?"

I felt almost as if I were back at my father's house, at one of his important society garden parties. I was quite good at small talk. I cleared my throat and tried again. "Isn't the weather temperate? I always find this time of year so charming."

Captain Tate gave me a perplexed look, and then pushed his shoulders back, nodding once and then shaking his head. It was as if he wanted to say something but had no idea how to.

Well, now he thought I was completely idiotic, so that was in some ways, beneficial. He wouldn't be pursuing me for any more dalliances if he thought I was a simple, shallow idiot.

I turned on my heel and hurried to my room to change.

My trousers were stiff with residue and it was starting to itch.

I peeled off the used clothes and tossed them in the corner of my cabin. I pulled fresh items of clothing out, allowing myself to briefly, longingly touch the fabric of my favourite and far too showy coat, which was of scarlet brocade. I had bought it from the market on impulse a few months ago and, although I seldom felt brave or confident in myself enough to wear it, I loved it. I couldn't have left it behind. Perhaps someday I'd feel the confidence in myself and put it on.

But for now, I pushed it to the bottom of my sea chest and hid it under the layers of less interesting clothing.

Another plain white shirt and brown, unflattering trousers would do for the ship.

The pirate ship. Mother, what have I done? What must you be thinking of me? I'll do better, I promise.

I glanced at her picture and then quickly away again, the shame and humiliation of my actions sinking over me like a heavy shroud.

Before I got dressed, I used a cloth and the water from my jug to clean myself off. While I cleaned myself I did my best to think of nothing but how good it felt to get the smell of another man off my skin.

Of course, thinking of that other man brought up certain, other thoughts. And memories. The sensation of his fingers on my skin. The way he had looked at me as if I were something previous, attractive, as if he couldn't resist me. It was a very pleasant thing to imagine, that someone might feel that way about me. And someone so handsome and strong as Tate, who was also so kind. And his body so fine...

Warmth pooled in my stomach as I remembered. The soft brush of his beard against my skin...

The size of his –

The door to my cabin slammed open and for a dreamy moment I wondered if I had summoned Captain Tate just from my wistful imaginings.

But it was Ezra.

I yelped and clutched my washcloth to my chest.

Very manly reaction, indeed. My father's voice scolded, inside my head.

Ezra's eyes widened and his gaze dropped down. In a rush to cover myself, I dropped the cloth, and had to snatch it up off the floor before I could hold it over my privates.

I suspected he had seen all the same. His eyes slowly dragged their way back up, taking in my chest, stomach, arms, every part of me laid bare before him.

He seemed to shake himself and tipped his chin up, looking away.

"Captain wants a word, when you're..." here he paused, intentionally. Carefully considering what word he could use to describe me. What collection of syllables could possibly sum me up? "More decent." He concluded, archly.

I felt, somehow, disappointed with this description. I wondered what I had expected from him instead?

I turned away from him but I could feel his eyes on me again. This time drinking in my nakedness from behind.

"Please close the door, Ezra," I said, with as much dignity as I could manage. I hoped he would take the hint and leave me alone. Instead, he closed the door, sealing us both inside in the tiny cabin.

I could hear him breathing behind me, moving closer.

My body was on high alert, and I felt I knew exactly where he was without looking, as if some part of me could sense him innately.

I was still absolutely bare and exposed so I reached for my trousers and started to step into them. Pulling them up as quickly as I could. I was afraid, but also my imagination – that terrible traitor – started to conjure images of what we could do.

The things Ezra and I could do while I was naked.

"I'm not -" Ezra stopped speaking as quickly as he had started. I felt the warmth of his breath as he moved closer to me. The heat of it sent a delicious shiver through my body, and I knew that whatever my confused mind was warring with, my body knew what it wanted, and it wanted Ezra. My body longed for his touch.

He had started to say something and not finished his sentence. I couldn't stand wondering what it was he seemed hesitant to express.

"What is it, that you are not?" I asked, my voice low and strained. Giving away some of my innermost feelings. My fingers fumbled, pulling my trousers closed over my growing hardness.

How humiliating.

The crew were soon going to think they'd picked up a common harlot, rather than a suitable cabin boy. At the rate I was having hot flashes and palpitations they may actually be right.

Perhaps Captain Tate had unleashed something inside of me? But these imaginings weren't necessarily new, they had simply lacked context. And the opportunity that being in close proximity to a lot of men afforded.

Now, it seemed that I had a certain amount of context, and the close attention of men on the ship, my imagination had expanded to new heights of daydream. And my body seemed more than happy, even eager to explore these dreams.

"I'm not accustomed to other men getting what I want," Ezra said. His voice was low but it was right in my ear. I could smell the hot mustiness of him. I shivered again.

"Oh? And uh, w-what do you want?" I asked. My voice was barely above a whisper but he was so close I knew he'd heard.

I asked him, although I feared I could guess his answer well enough.

Instead of answering, he pressed something hard into my back. At first I thought it was a knife or dagger and I went still, afraid. But the touch proved so gentle, and somehow warm – he scratched down and I realised it was a fingernail. He touched it to the arch of my right shoulder blade, and scratched a line down towards my hips and my ass.

It took perhaps five seconds all told, but every nerve in my body paid attention to the sensation. It seemed to take far longer than that. The feeling both gentle and rough enough to put me on edge. My breath caught and heat pooled at the base of my abdomen. I held my breath until his fingernail withdrew from my skin.

He cleared his throat, turned and left the cabin.

He slammed the door open so hard it banged on the wall and stood ajar.

I took a deep breath, gathering myself. Trying to regain some semblance of functionality. A noise startled me and I turned to see Zeb the cat, scratching at the door frame before sauntering into the cabin. He gave me an unimpressed look and jumped on the bed, seemingly to get a better look at me.

"What was all that about, do you think?" I asked him.

If a cat could shrug its shoulders, I felt that Zeb would have done so then. Instead he gazed at me steadily and twitched his whiskers.

"You're no help."

I picked my looking glass out and examined myself. The bruise – or love bite, as Ezra had named it – bloomed purple and brown on my neck. It was much larger than I had expected it to be. A large, clear sign for all to see and I was at a loss for how to cover it.

I tried to twist about, putting the glass behind me to see my own back. Ezra had scratched me lightly but I still felt the places he'd touched as if it may have left a mark, similar to Captain Tate's.

I wasn't sure, as I turned and tried to peer over my own shoulder, if there was a red line, or if I was just fooling myself.

Did I want there to be a mark?

No. Of course not.

Ezra was a pirate, just the same as Tate.

Tate.

He wanted to speak to me. I couldn't put that off, much as I might wish to.

My stomach dropping rapidly, I pulled on my shirt and found a light cotton scarf that I tied as a cravat. It did well enough at hiding the mark on my throat, but it was an obvious disguise and I was sure the crew would notice. No one else on the ship wore a cravat.

But I'd rather feel overdressed than have everyone staring at the bruise and knowing what had gone on.

Better a dandy than the Captain's whore, yes?

Even as I thought it, I felt I was betraying him. Tate had been charming, gentle, and kind. It had been a wonderful experience and here I was ashamed of it because of his career.

But his being a pirate was terrifying, that was still true.

I left the cravat in place, and steeled myself before leaving the cabin to find him again.

I'd speak to him as briefly as possible and come back to my room to hide.

CHAPTER TWELVE - IN WHICH
GIDEON STOPS AVOIDING TATE

Captain Tate stood at the helm, and as I approached him I had to admit he cut a truly impressive figure. His shoulders were squared and strong, and he stood at his full height, both hands on the wheel. A white cotton shirt unlaced down half his chest. His long hair blowing behind him.

My mouth went dry as I moved up beside him.

"Captain," I said, softly. I pressed my hands together behind my back, trying to ignore all the feelings and things that had passed between us and focus on being a factotum. "You wished to speak with me?"

"I'm sorry, Aaron," he said. His voice low. "For what happened. I'm sorry you didn't know that we're – I'm a pirate." He spoke the words fast, and I supposed it wouldn't do for the captain of a pirate ship to go around apologising to people.

I tried to formulate a response. The standard garden party politeness wouldn't help me now. The Captain was being straightforward and speaking the truth so I should do the same.

"Thank you for your apology," I said, matching his volume. "I...I must admit I was deeply shocked, and with the new information that I understand now, I would request you release me from my contract and allow me to disembark at the ship's next port."

I didn't look at him as I made this request, instead I looked straight ahead. But out of the corner of my eye I saw movement. Tate had looked sharply at me and then ahead again.

There was a pause, then he said thoughtfully. "The first port?" he showed no emotion, and my stomach sank unpleasantly. I realised that some part of me had hoped he would express disappointment or perhaps ask me to stay aboard. But why should he do that? And why should I feel cheated that he wasn't upset?

I had told him I wasn't interested, so there's no reason for me to expect he'd pursue me.

My head was full of confusion but actually, more precisely the confusion was in my heart. My head didn't understand what my heart wanted.

Running away from home had skewed my senses. I wasn't used to making my own life decisions and I was no good at it.

"Yes, the first *safe* port," I added. I imagined the raucous and lawless ports described in my novels and suppressed a shudder. I wouldn't want to end up in one of *those* dens of inequity.

Or would I?

The part of me that couldn't stop picturing Captain Tate naked, or remembering how good the sex was needled at my attention.

I told it to be quiet. It would not.

My cheeks warmed and I looked away so the Captain wouldn't notice. Unfortunately, the new direction of my gaze happened to direct me exactly at the spot Ezra was working. He was hauling on a rope, his face tilted up displaying his exquisite jawline. He had shed his shirt and stood with his feet braced on the deck, I was surprised to see a tattoo on his back, a black bird of some kind, perhaps a crow or a raven, its wings spread over his shoulder blades, almost as if he were some kind of fallen angel with feathered wings.

The tattoo seemed to move as the muscles of his back rippled and flexed under his olive skin.

My mouth watered and that annoying part of me spoke up again.

He's delicious. I want to do so many things with him. Have him do things to me.

Ezra looked over at me suddenly and I quickly whipped my head to the front. My cheeks were certainly blazing now. I cursed my fair complexion and the way it revealed my innermost thoughts.

Beside me, the Captain cleared his throat.

"Well, Gideon- "

"Aaron," I said quickly.

The last thing I need is a bunch of pirates knowing who I really am.

"Aaron, of course. Well, I suppose we could find you a safe port, perhaps towards Panama or the Americas. It will be around ten days sailing, assuming fine weather. We have to avoid the Splintered Islands."

"I'm sorry, I'm not familiar with the..." I paused, unsure if I had heard him right. "The Splintered Islands?" I swallowed. I had forgotten my station. "I mean, sorry, Captain."

Captain Tate looked at me and I returned his gaze. He gave me a fleeting but warm smile. Enough to set my foolish heart fluttering all over again.

"Aye, the Splintered Isles. There's things there which are best avoided, lad. Very bad luck."

"I've not heard of them," I said. I frowned, I had thought I knew the basics of geography around this area.

"Aye, I gathered that much." He sounded amused.

"Ten days, and then you'll let me off?" I asked.

"You have my word," Tate said. "Though I hope you know," he seemed to stop himself. I looked into his eyes and bit my lip, there was emotion there that I wasn't ready to face. I gave him a tiny nod, as if he needed my permission to continue speaking.

"I hope you know that I'll be sad to see you leave."

My heart thudded against my ribs and I felt a sudden sadness. "Yes, well, uh. Was there anything else you'd like me to do for you, this day?"

I blushed *again* realising how that sentence could sound like an invitation to something salacious rather than just enquiring about my job.

Tate gazed at me, and his melancholy evaporated, replaced by a smile I could only describe as roguish.

"Aye. Change my bedclothes for me," he said.

Fuming, and certain now that the skin of my cheeks matched the flaming redness of my hair, I marched into the Captain's cabin and gathered up the sheets.

The same sheets he and I had soiled together.

They smelled of sweat, of Tate and myself, and the...

Humiliating.

He'd done this on purpose.

I was incensed at the indignity of it, and my traitorous body was aroused which just made the job harder to do, which made me frustrated.

Being back in his cabin, where we had shared such intimacies, smelling the sheets – the evidence of what we had done, and all the memories it brought back. It was almost too much for me.

I bundled them roughly in my arms and went below deck to exchange them for fresh linen.

It was a small mercy, I suppose, that I had at least picked up the fresh sheets and left the soiled ones to be washed when I ran into Ezra. I was climbing up the narrow stairway, my mind already on my escape to my own cabin and a moment's respite, when Ezra blocked the way. He descended from the deck.

There wasn't room in that space for two people, but I didn't want to back up. It would appear cowardly to him, I was sure. He already thought little enough of me.

I tried to hold my ground, but Ezra didn't break his stride. His dark eyes glinted in the low light as he advanced on me.

My bravado failed and I pressed my back to the wall, clutching the sheets to my chest to make myself as out of the way as possible.

He brushed against me, his breath briefly in my face, hot and spicy. Not unpleasantly, the scent brought to mind oranges, fresh from the market.

I inhaled as he pushed past, jostling me hard enough that I almost lost my grip on the bedclothes.

"Well, I never," I huffed but - coward that I am - I waited until I was safely above deck and him far below.

I kept my head down and myself to myself for two days.

I ate quickly with the crew and retired to my cabin as often as possible. I set a comfortable rhythm as I thought of the days ahead and how I would soon be leaving the Grey Kelpie. A thought that was both exciting and more desolate than I had expected.

The world outside the ship, outside Kingston was utterly unknown and I had no idea what I would do in whatever port Tate dropped me off in.

Best not to worry about it until it happens.

Each night I went to bed early, and Zeb would yowl to be let in until I relented, and he would sleep snug in the bend of my knees or leaning against my stomach.

I spoke to the Captain only insofar as he had jobs for me – which was rarely after the sheets incident – he seemed to be content to let me avoid him.

I wanted to be somewhat useful even if I was leaving so I assigned myself the task of taking stock of the cargo and food supplies.

The daily log was well kept with the day to day minutiae, but I suspected the bigger picture was missing. I hunted below deck for chests and boxes in hidden corners. Things that hadn't been opened for a while. I found some strange wooden dolls in one box and noted them down. A vase packed in straw in a box wedged under an unused bunk, and a sea chest with some clothing in it which all appeared to be child's sizes. Very peculiar.

I had been working a few hours that particular day, until my stomach started to rumble.

The galley was my first stop for food, but it was uncharacteristically empty of people. Curious, I continued upwards.

Heading upstairs into the bright sunlight, I had to pause for a moment as my eyes adjusted. My lungs happy to have fresh air again.

The mood on the deck was curiously light, almost festive. There was laughter, and – aside from the helmsman – it seemed the entire crew was lining the side of the ship and looking overboard on the Starboard side.

"Can you see them?"

"Aye, I'm not blind, Shem!"

"Not often you see- "

"Whatever is everyone looking at?" I asked, but there was no answer, no one could hear me unless I shouted and I didn't want to draw attention to myself. Instead, I joined the edge of the crowd, braced my hands on the edge of the boat and looked into the water.

The swells of the ocean were chopped into pieces. White foam and miniature waves here and there, and the sleek grey bodies causing all this disturbance.

Dolphins.

They broke the water here and there, making a huffing noise as they sprayed air and water out of their blowholes.

"Oh," I breathed, quite enchanted by the sight. Dolphins did come into Kingston harbour sometimes but I had never been this close to them. It almost seemed if I leaned over and reached out one might touch my fingers.

I stayed with both hands on the side of the boat.

As I watched, a dolphin breached the water and arced through the air. The beast was beautiful. A clean, shiny hide, a sparkling eye and a mouth smiling wide, as if it leapt for pure joy. Perhaps it did.

I wish I could feel so free, so joyful, simply for living.

It dove back into the water with barely a splash and another jumped a few yards from the side of the ship.

The crew cheered.

I laughed aloud, astounded first that the dolphins were there, and second, that the captain would allow this kind of behaviour.

Leaning against the railings I watched and felt my mouth tug into a smile. The expression felt strange, as if I hadn't smiled for several days – which I suppose was true. With all the things that had happened with Tate, and avoiding Ezra, keeping my head down and busying myself with working, I hadn't exactly been enjoying myself.

But this?

This was everything wonderful about sailing the ocean. The sunlight warmed my shoulders and as I watched the sea creatures at play, I felt a serenity settle over me like a mantle.

I had a certain sensation that this was where I was supposed to be. The boom creaked against the mast with wind, the temperate air was scented with salt spray and the wonders of the ocean were showing themselves to me.

The man beside me on the railings shifted and I saw with a start that it was Ezra. His elbow pressed against mine, but he hadn't seemed to notice it was me.

But while he hadn't realised, I allowed myself an indulgent moment to admire his profile. His jawline was fine from this angle, the short, manicured stubble accentuating his bone structure.

He was exceptionally handsome, and for a moment I wondered idly if he or the Captain were more handsome.

But I dismissed the idea.

Both were handsome in different ways.

And both a little frightening, or perhaps... perhaps I should say thrilling since I wasn't actually afraid either of them would hurt me.

The Captain looked frightening until you got to know him. I couldn't find him scary at all now, although he was definitely still impressive.

I looked around and immediately spotted Captain Tate, he was at the prow of the ship, leaning over and calling to the dolphins as though they were long lost friends.

Returning my gaze to Ezra, I considered his profile once more. He looked a little like a wolf in human form. Wiry, muscular, slightly pointy of feature but attractive and desirable.

I felt my mouth water, remembering how he had looked with no shirt on.

"Beautiful," I breathed.

Ezra nodded. "Aye, it is, isn't it. Sort of strange how some things even I can't get jaded about."

I flushed, thankful that at least he'd thought I was speaking about the dolphins and not him.

His voice was different, still gravelly and rough, sexy, the edge of something deliciously exciting, but it was softer. I could tell then – the affection he had for the sea and the creatures in it. It mirrored my own. The love he bore for the whole career of sailing was now utterly obvious to me.

Why would you choose this life if you didn't love it?

He looked up at me sidelong and his face closed up.

There was a pang in my chest.

I had ruined his joy. I had upset this beautiful, infuriating man. How could I put it right? I had to say something.

As I was leaving the ship soon, it felt like my responsibility to set things to rights. I would speak to him now. Maybe it was the miracle of the dolphins giving me the courage to bridge the incalculable gap between us.

"I'm sorry," I said.

Ezra looked at me sharply and his jaw tightened again. I could see a muscle pulsing in his neck. He looked towards the front of the ship and then turned back to the view of the dolphins.

My stomach tightened. Surely I hadn't made things worse? I hoped I hadn't.

Ezra let out a growling, frustrated sigh. Then he pushed back from the railing with both hands and barked at the crew, the sudden noise causing me and several others to startle.

"Back to work! Not like you've never seen a pod of dolphins before."

The men scattered, some grumbling and some calling out. "Aye, Ezra!"

Captain Tate straightened up and went to Ezra, the two of them immediately starting a conversation about the weather, winds and tides and walking away.

I licked my lips.

I realised that since he had woken me down by the brig, there had been a yearning in me to make things right with Ezra. I don't know entirely why it mattered so much, but I found the thought of him angry with me unbearable. Abhorrent.

But I also knew enough not to push my luck right then.

I would keep my distance a little while longer. Unfortunately, avoiding him and the Captain left me less and less of the ship to occupy.

CHAPTER THIRTEEN - IN WHICH GIDEON IS TIED UP

Two nights had passed since the dolphins had visited the ship. I had gone to bed early both evenings and told my every inner thought to Zeb the cat – the loneliness, the confusion, the desire to set things right with Ezra. Although I tried to pitch my voice lower, so that Tate if he were in his cabin, didn't overhear, but it was hard to remember to be quiet when I got deep into my own feelings.

Zeb had listened patiently and settled to sleep on my chest both nights.

I was headed down below deck to do another sweep for anything I may have previously missed while taking stock before. Although I knew I had been thorough – as I had plenty of time avoiding people to devote to the work.

I found nothing new. I considered, finally, going to visit Sagorika, just for someone to talk to who wasn't the ship's cat.

Sagorika was unlikely to confuse me the same way Ezra and Tate did.

"Right, well," I said, by way of motivating myself to head towards her cabin.

There was a sound behind me – a footstep. I turned towards the stairwell and there stood Ezra, his jaw tight, his eyes sparkling in the low light.

"Ezra," I breathed.

"Aaron," he said. He ran a hand through the longer hair on top of his head. "There you are. I've been looking for you."

"You have? W-why? Is there something you needed?"

Technically I am factotum to the Captain but of course the First Mate could call on me as well. Perhaps he had some job that needed doing.

"Aaron, you are driving me to distraction," he said.

That was unexpected.

My eyebrows shot up and I coughed involuntarily.

"I, um, I'm sorry, what was that?"

Ezra took three steps and suddenly he was inches from me. I looked into his eyes and I forgot how to breathe. Somehow, I could breathe in only, and breathing out was impossible.

"I'm afraid I don't understand." My voice came out somewhat strained.

"Ever since I saw you, in your cabin, without your clothes," Ezra growled. Then he shook his head. "No, before that. You're an absolute mystery to me, and I can't abide mysteries. They hound my mind until I unravel them. I want you, Aaron."

Unravel? Hounding? He wants me? None of this made any sense.

Breathing was harder still. There was no air in this room, I tugged at the collar of my shirt, which was done up far too tight. I needed to get some fresh air and fast.

Ezra peered into my eyes. It was if he were searching for something.

Good Lord, he probably wanted me to respond, didn't he? But I had no idea what to say. My years of etiquette kicked in.

"That's so kind of you to say," I replied. Then I cringed. I sounded like a student at a finishing school. I should spread my skirts and curtsey next, or flutter my fan. If I had skirts or a fan, of course. Which I didn't.

"Christ on a cross," he swore. He shook his head slowly back and forth, like a dog – *or a wolf*. "Well, do you want me, too? The Captain hasn't been by your cabin in days."

"No," I said, quickly. "He hasn't."

Then I wondered why I had been so quick to assure him of that fact. I felt as if I were denying myself something.

Pretending I didn't want something when I did... And Ezra was more than a sugar cake on a platter. He was flesh and blood, and I wanted him. And for some unknown reason he wanted me too. I should probably take advantage of that while it was true. But it was hard to speak.

"So, what do you say?" he pressed. "I've seen the way you look at me, well, I want you, too."

I lost the ability to breathe all over again. I was in danger of fainting.

"The way I look at you?" I murmured.

My eyes seemed suddenly keen as an eagle's. I could see the gentle swell of his lower lip, I could smell the salt on his skin. I could sense his warmth only inches from me.

My mind flooded with images of Ezra with no shirt on, his muscles and the tattoo...

How could I lie to him?

How could I lie to myself?

I couldn't.

"Y-yes, I do," I said. It was barely above a whisper, but he was so close to me he heard it.

Ezra's mouth quirked up at one side and he closed the short

distance between us. He crashed his mouth onto mine and I met him like the sand dunes meet the crashing waves. Catching, working together, naturally meant to be in concert.

It wasn't like the kiss I had shared with Tate. That had been soft, gentle, almost kind. This kiss felt more like duel. Like he was challenging me to something and I could either fight back or surrender.

But which to choose?

Ezra pushed against me, crowding me back against the wooden wall behind me. My back hit the hard surface and I gasped into the kiss.

Ezra's lips curled against mine in a smile or a snarl and I knew I didn't want to fight back, I didn't want to challenge this man. I wanted, more than anything in that moment, to make him happy.

I reached up to put my arms around his neck the way I had with Tate, wanting to be closer, but he took hold of my wrists and pulled my arms up over my head.

I squirmed, pinned between him and the wall at my back. "Wh-what are you doing?"

"Keeping you in your place," Ezra growled. He bared his teeth - wolf like - and a shiver coursed up my spine. "You are going to take what I give you."

I nodded. No desire to fight back, just to make him happy. To enjoy whatever he had planned.

"I want to make you mine." He leaned in close, his lips brushing my jaw so softly it was a ghost of a tease and I strained against his hold, trying to claim his lips but he held me fast.

I whimpered softly, wanting him to let me go so I could touch and kiss him, but also on fire with the enforced denial of it. Ezra was in control and I was willing to let him have it.

"How does it feel?" he growled. He tilted his head and his lips found the spot on my neck the captain had marked. The bruise had largely faded, but his teeth closed on my skin and he worked to bring it out again. The sting of his mouth on that spot flooded heat through my body.

I tried to answer him but my moans obscured my words. "It feels - ohhhhh..." He pulled back and fixed me with a stern look.

"Tell me, now, if you want me to claim you. Do you want to be mine, Aaron?"

"Yes," I said, as quickly as I could between groans. "And call me Gideon, my name is Gideon." I tried to thrust my hips forward to grind against him, but his grip tightened on my wrists.

"Gideon?" His eyebrows raised and he smirked. "We'll talk about that later. But if you can't behave..." Ezra produced a length of rope from his pocket. He yanked my hands down in front of me and and swiftly wrapped the rope several times around my wrists, tying it off in between.

My desire for him burned brighter still. I looked up at him to ask questions but he crashed his mouth against mine and it was all I could do to return the kiss. I was so hungry for him, so desperate to feel him against me.

He took hold of the rope holding me and tugged my arms up over my head again, looping the rope end over a lantern hook buried in the wall.

"There, that ought to keep you still," he growled. With both his hands free, he went to work on undressing me, pulling my shirt open and running his rough hands over the bare skin of my chest and stomach.

He tugged my trousers open and then down, and my skin thrilled to feel his hands over my hips and thighs.

I wanted to feel his hands on my most private parts but he seemed to be intentionally avoiding them. Teasing me with his hands. His mouth moving down from my neck to kiss and then nip at my shoulder. The skin there felt paper-thin, and every part of me ached for more of his attention.

I felt quite desperate for it, in fact.

"Please," I managed to gasp out. "Please..."

"Please what?" he growled. In the back of my mind I realised he was enjoying teasing me in this manner, that he was doing it on purpose to drive me to distraction.

Well, of course he was. He had done all this intentionally after all. The ropes, the roughness of his teeth and his hands.

I gasped again. "Please, touch me," I breathed.

"I am touching you," he drawled. His fingers pinched the inside of my thigh and I jumped, crying out.

"That hurt," I protested. But my indignation faded into something else, as he rubbed his finger over the pinched place and my body melted into the pleasure of his touch. "Ohhh."

"I suspected you'd be a little wench about pain." He pulled back to watch my face and pinched me again on the other thigh this time, again I jolted and then moaned, my body translating the sharp sting into warm heat. "I like being right."

My face was burning red - the humiliation of him guessing that for some reason my body would interpret pain as pleasure - the fact that I was exposed, bare in front of him, helpless with my hands tied and practically begging him to do more to me.

It was all deliciously *wrong* and I couldn't get enough of it. I felt I should communicate this all to him, somehow.

"Please, more," I said without thinking. It wasn't exactly eloquent but he seemed to understand what it was I meant.

He grinned, gripped me by the hips and flipped me around. I

was now facing the wooden wall. He shoved my legs apart, and I felt even more his prisoner, helpless to stop him - he could do whatever he wished to my body.

That probably shouldn't arouse me as much as it does. Being the prisoner of a murderous pirate. But he wasn't planning to murder me, unless it was through teasing and arousal.

Could one die from that?

I was panting so hard my tongue was dry and I closed my eyes, losing myself, indulging in the luxury of not having to make any decisions. Whatever Ezra wished to happen would happen, and I was confident that it would be pleasurable indeed.

His fingers parted my arse cheeks and I gasped again, feeling him teasing me there. His finger slick with spit or with the special oil the Captain had in his cabin.

I moaned again, wordless, but even to my own ears I sounded wanton and needy.

"That's a good boy, Gideon." He pressed his chest against my back. The fabric of his shirt seemed to be another pleasurable touch on my fevered skin. "That's good, just relax for me and it will feel so good for both of us..."

I nodded a little, letting my forehead drop forward to press against the wood as he stretched me with surprisingly gentle fingers. I came open for him easily, it seemed, as he kept on murmuring praise to me.

For my part, I was panting and moaning, every new thing he did to me seemed to be the most delicious thing I had experienced, and I was greedy for more. Some incredible hunger in me was awakened and my sense of dignity was entirely gone. I just wanted more.

Finally his fingers withdrew and I felt something larger but smoother tease me. His cock felt velvety soft and I felt hungry all over again.

"Are you ready for this, pet?" He growled, his teeth catching the shell of my ear and worrying at it.

Did he just call me his pet?

I gasped and nodded, a stilted, aborted movement as I didn't care to tug my ear out of the grip his teeth had on it.

He pushed inside me.

I remembered how when I had filled the Captain I had felt powerful, complete. This was a different form of completeness. As if I had always yearned for something to make me whole and now Ezra was giving it to me.

He wrapped an arm around my waist, gasping into my ear. "You're so tight Aa- Gideon," he said. His voice cracked.

His voice... Was it possible I was affecting him? He wanted me so much it was... affecting him that deeply? Warmth spread through my chest and despite the ropes around my arms, and the arm around my waist, the fact of him filling me - taking what he wanted - I felt powerful.

He desired *me* as much as I desired him?

I groaned loud enough I felt the whole ship must hear it.

Behind me, Ezra started to move his hips. The slip and drag of him inside me was enough that I almost climaxed on the spot. I bucked and gasped and Ezra closed his hand around my cock, his forefinger and thumb closing in a tight ring around the base of me.

"Uh uh," he growled. "Not until I give you permission, pet."

My entire body flushed hot and I whimpered, squirming back against his body. Was that a thing that he could do? Hold back my climax until he willed it? The ring of his fingers around me certainly felt definitive, holding me in place.

His hips shifted again, and again I lost my thoughts to the sensation of the drag and pull, the slick deliciousness of his cock inside of me. I was in a state of utter bliss.

He increased the speed of his hip movements, grunting and panting in my ear as he fucked me hard. If my mouth hadn't been hanging open I imagine it would have rattled my teeth, but as it was I was panting like a dog.

He held me close against his chest with one hand, the other clamped around my cock as he pounded into me, and all too soon he was moaning, approaching climax. His hand on my cock loosened and stroked me instead.

"Now, pet," he grunted in my ear. "Come for me, now!"

My body had been boiling - stuck on the precipice for far too long - and now as he said those words, and pumped his hand over my cock, I came without any further warning.

I felt him throb inside me at almost the same instant and we moaned together.

I slumped forward in his hold, I became aware of an aching sting in my wrists as I put more of my weight on the ropes.

Ezra murmured to me. "Did so well... what a good boy... perfect... so good and tight."

My body was flooded with the heat of climax and now I felt as if I were glowing from the sweetness of his words. How could he be so harsh with his body and then so gentle with his words? It was absolutely intoxicating.

He pulled out and my knees went weak.

I felt half in a dream as he reached up and undid the ropes and his arm became even tighter around me as I failed to hold myself up.

"Come on," he said, gently, and tugged me over to the

wooden bench, where he pulled me into his lap, his arms circling me, holding me upright as I recovered.

After several long minutes of heart fluttering and gentle trembling, my head cleared, and I was able to come back to my body - feel the parts of me that stung or were comfortably worn out.

"That was unbelievable," I managed to say. A small part of me twisted inside, what we'd just done was more than just sinful, wasn't it? It was... perverted. But I couldn't deny that I'd enjoyed it all the same.

What does that make me?

"I'm glad you thought so," Ezra said. He cleared his throat, looked me square in the eye. "Are you, uh, are you hurt at all?"

I shook my head. "Just a little bruised," I said. "Not much worse than after I..." I had been about to bring up Tate, but that seemed like a poor idea. Ezra seemed to catch my meaning all the same. A thunderous expression flashed across his face and he looked away. I could feel his arms tensing around me.

"We should get back to work," he said. He shifted me off his lap and got up, pulling his clothes back on and into order.

I had to say something to make it right - things with Ezra had been so good and right briefly, and now this - but my mouth was dry and my mind empty. I couldn't pretend Tate and I hadn't shared something, Ezra and I both knew we had. And now Ezra and I had...

Done all that.

A small and exquisite pain started behind my left temple as Ezra quickly vacated the room and went above decks.

I have made everything worse, again.

CHAPTER FOURTEEN - IN WHICH GIDEON TRIES TO PRETEND THINGS ARE FINE

There didn't seem to be much point in hiding below decks after that incident. Or rather, I could have continued in my busywork, but the feeling - or perhaps fear - that Ezra and Tate could be talking to each other about me, kept me from it.

I couldn't be responsible for any kind of rift or resentment between the Captain or the First Mate, after all. I was planning on leaving the ship, and I was resolute about sticking to that plan.

I hung around, getting in the way more often than not, for the rest of the day, my shirt collar turned up in an effort to conceal the bruise I was sure Ezra had left on my throat.

That night I told Zeb everything that had happened, as had become my nightly ritual. He seemed unimpressed, until I scratched him under the chin. Then he slept on my chest, which was both physically uncomfortable and deeply comforting.

The next day Captain Tate threw a party instead of our standard dinner on the ship.

"Attention, all!" He called, in the mid afternoon. "Tonight

we're celebrating, got a little extra food, and we're about to head past the Splintered Isles."

The man beside me folded his arms and groaned. "Why are we going past there?" His name was Joseph, I thought. I'd exchanged only a few words with him, but he seemed to be all right.

"What is so frightening about the Splintered Isles?" I asked.

Joseph shook his head and shuddered. "Cursed, they are, a place of ill luck. Sailing close to them invites wickedness onto the ship."

"We're headed to a safe port and this is the quickest way," Tate said. His eyes landed on me and his expression became inscrutable. He looked away again.

I felt my face flush and my hand moved to cover the damned bruise on my neck. How could I continue to be so indecorous? I should have put the cravat back on.

"The point is, we're anchoring and having a shindig tonight," Tate said. "So let's hear a cheer, you old scallywags!"

The crew let loose a deafening cheer.

As the crowd broke into smaller groups, and some started rolling out barrels of wine and ale, I sidled past as quickly as I could and went towards my cabin. I sneaked inside and shut the door fast behind me.

The last thing I needed was to be hanging around both Ezra and Tate while they were drinking. What if they got in a fight? It'd be humiliating on so many levels: as if I were a maiden in need of defending. I blushed, because whatever words one might use for me, maiden was not at all accurate, now.

But it would also let the crew know what was going on, and then I'd be the Captain's whore - or the first mate's. I couldn't stand the idea of everyone knowing my business.

Zeb the cat was sleeping on my bed, stretched out to his full, and rather considerable length.

"Excuse me," I said. "This is my room, you shall have to move."

For a cat that had appeared to be completely asleep, Zeb was quick to swipe a paw at me, claws out and all. I pulled my hand back. He growled, which was very un-Zeb-like behaviour.

"Zeb, move!" I reached towards him, trying to slip a hand under him to scoop him up but he hissed and swiped at me, his back feet kicking and his claws out.

I stepped back and folded my arms. "What on Earth has got into you, Zeb?"

He eyed me balefully and then rolled onto his back, looking for all the world like an innocent kitten with a beautiful fluffy belly.

I reached towards him and brushed my fingers against the ridiculously soft fur of his underbelly and he fastened himself to my arm with all four paws and his teeth.

"Zeb!" I cried out at the sudden pain as multitudes of claws sunk into my skin. I couldn't shake my hand to free myself, or he'd have sunk the claws in deeper, so I went as still as possible until he let go and then I slowly backed away, nursing my poor torn hand and wrist.

On inspection I had several angry red scratches, but I wasn't losing blood or anything dire.

I pouted at Zeb.

"That was cruel."

Zeb blinked at me and rolled on his back again, his head tilted in a very endearing manner. "No, I see this for what it is now, a trap, and I will not fall for it."

I glanced at the picture of my mother and sighed. I could almost hear her voice in my head.

Go and spend time with the crew, Gideon, it's good for you to be with people. Don't hide yourself away in fear.

I sighed heavily, pulled out my scarlet coat and shrugged it on. I was already going to be ridiculously conspicuous, I may as well be conspicuous in my favourite coat.

I ran a brush through my hair and pulled it back more neatly, as if I were preparing for one of my father's parties rather than a drunken revel on the decks of a pirate ship.

Also, taking time with my appearance made me feel a little less dirty, and a little more myself. I had told both Ezra and Tate my true name, I wonder if they had discussed that. I wondered if they had discussed me at all, and blushed deep enough to match the scarlet fabric of my coat.

Mustn't think about that, I told myself. *Just keep your head up and maintain some kind of dignity.*

CHAPTER FIFTEEN - IN WHICH GIDEON TRIES RUM

I strode out of my cabin and onto the deck.

Dignity.

There was a low whistle and I looked over to see Sagorika watching me. She nodded and raised her cup in salute. "Nice coat!"

Relieved, I walked towards her. "Thank you kindly." I sat beside her on a makeshift bench of wooden boxes and she leaned her shoulder against mine. Sagorika was a safe person to speak to, I felt comfortable in her presence.

"Did you get a drink, Aaron?"

I shook my head. "I don't need one, I'm all right."

"Nonsense!" She cried. "We're sailing close to the Splintered Isles, you must drink! It could be your last chance for all we know!"

She reached to the side and pulled out a bottle, handing it to me. "What about a cup?"

"Just drink from the bottle, fancy boy, it'll do just as well."

My cheeks warmed slightly from the nickname, but I

supposed I had invited it with the coat. Besides, it was a better nickname than some others I'd probably earned.

I swallowed, wiped the mouth of the bottle with my hand and then took a drink.

The wine was surprisingly good, sweet and slightly dry. I drank again, enjoying the sensation of warmth spreading down my chest.

"What actually are the Splintered Isles?" I asked. "Joseph said it was ill news but not much else."

Sagorika draped her arm over my shoulders. "The Splintered Isles is more than ill news, it is an ill land. A place of curses and cursed beings," she said.

I shuddered involuntarily. "Cursed beings? You mean like, witches? Or something worse?"

"Aye, there's a witch there all right, and he's got no amount of fondness for our ship. Or our Captain, more to the point."

"Pardon?" I took another drink of wine and suppressed a burp. "Why our ship in particular?"

"I'm not entirely sure of the story, fancy boy, but there's rumours. Rumours that Tate and the witch used to be close, friends or lovers, the stories vary. In some of them they sailed together on this very ship, with the witch - Solomon, his name is - providing fair winds and fine weather to aid the ship along. Together they brought down a whole company of slavers, they say. Freed the slaves, gave them the ships they'd been imprisoned on and tossed the slavers into the sea for the monsters that Solomon called up. They took the profits from the slavers and made a fine career of it."

I could almost imagine it. Tate at the helm with a dashing sea witch beside him, the two of them lovers, kissing under the moonlight, the waves urging the ship along to wherever they would sail to next. Something tugged at my memory - Tate mentioning that he'd once had a partner...

"Whatever happened?"

"They fell out," Sagorika pitched her voice louder and I realised with a start that a few more of the crew had gathered around. Sitting on the deck and leaning on masts to listen to Sagorika speak. In the back of my mind I wondered if I oughtn't move out from under her arm, but I was comfortable enough, and her fingers were tight on my shoulder, encouraging me to stay.

"They fell out. Some say it was a lover's quarrel, perhaps the Captain was unfaithful, perhaps the witch was. Perhaps two men of such ambition were never meant to get along for as long as they did. Some say Tate cheated Solomon out of a fine bounty, and some say that witches are fickle, inconstant creatures and one day Solomon hexed the captain."

"That'll be it!" Shem, a crewman said, laughing. "Tate probably tossed a special stone overboard and the witch missed it."

"As I say, none of us know the truth of it," Sagorika continued, fixing Shem with a severe look. "But they were enemies from that day. Tate cast Solomon off the ship and onto the Splintered Isles and left him there. Any time the Grey Kelpie sails within a league of those islands Solomon can see and hear us, and his curses could reach us. So, we are cautious. We never go too close, and any time we do, we celebrate our lives the night before, just in case."

Sagorika's voice pitched lower and then she pulled her arm from around me and clapped twice. "And that's the tale."

The crew made noises of approval, cheering and toasting Sagorika with their drinks.

"A fine story!"

"An excellent storyteller!"

"Why go near them at all?" I asked. "Surely we can navigate without going close to that particular part of the ocean."

"Aye, we could, but it's in an inconvenient place to avoid," Sagorika said. "The route past there is often free of the English Navy, and much quicker sailing for it. Besides that, it's on our way to the port Tate was considering."

"Hm," I said. I tapped my chin with one finger.

Something about the plan didn't seem right to me, surely there were other ways to go rather than directly past an island a witch with a vendetta dwelled on?

"I think Tate likes to tease him, honestly," a familiar gravelly voice said. With a start I noticed Ezra, he'd been skulking at the edge of the group and I had no idea how long he'd been there.

"Tease... him..." I repeated, my voice more breath than sound. It had barely been two hours since Ezra had taught me what teasing truly was and my body prickled pleasantly at the memory.

"Aye, sail past with his ship looking all pristine and profitable, remind the witch of what he's lost. I wouldn't put it past the captain, not for one moment."

The other assembled crew laughed and jeered and agreed and I allowed myself a terribly indulgent moment looking at Ezra while he joked with the other crew. His attention was directed away from me for the moment.

He was handsome as ever, but more than that, he appeared relaxed, happy in himself in a way I hadn't seen before. His grin was undoubtedly roguish, but I found it alluring rather than alarming.

Was it possible that having his way with me had eased something inside him? No, I was giving myself far too much credit.

"The fact of the matter is," Sagorika said, getting everyone's attention back on her. "No one knows for sure what happened with the sea witch and the captain, but just in case, we drink, we celebrate life, and we make our peace with what's to come."

I stole another glance at Ezra and found him staring back at me openly, his expression hungry. I felt naked again, and I quickly looked away. I lifted the wine bottle to my lips and drained it, longing suddenly for some sort of dulling of the senses so that I wasn't feeling everything quite so intensely.

The more wine I had in me, the easier Father's parties had been. My anxiety would ease, I would find it easier to talk to strangers and I felt affection grow in my heart for the people around me.

That afternoon was no exception. In fact, I probably needed more than at one of Father's parties, given the presence of Ezra and Captain Tate.

I got up as several of the crew moved away - Sagorika's story was over, and there was no need for them to hang about. I avoided Ezra and went in search of more wine. It wasn't hard to find, and soon I had both hands wrapped around a generous sized mug of wine straight from the barrel.

"How's things with you?" Tate said, appearing beside me. "You have a very lovely coat on."

"Oh, it's uh, well," I stammered. "Thank you."

I looked up at him and smiled, because although none of the problems had been solved, he was a warm and handsome man, and I liked him. And I really liked my coat. It was red satin brocade and it had cost a pretty penny. My father had rolled his eyes when he saw how much I had paid for it.

I leaned back against the ship's railing and he mirrored my position, leaning up beside me. "Enjoying the wine, are you?" he asked.

"Yes," I said. "Wine makes things easier, don't you find?"

"I suppose I do," he said. "Prefer rum myself."

"I've never had rum."

He offered me his cup. "Try it if you like?"

I took the cup from him and sniffed tentatively. It smelled like Tate; warm and spicy. I took a sip and coughed at the acrid taste of it, but it warmed me on the way down in a rather delicious way. I handed him the cup back. "Rather interesting, isn't it?"

Tate laughed and raised his eyebrows. "I guess it is at that, Gideon."

"You're supposed to call me Aaron, when we're not in private," I said. I prodded his arm with my finger, emboldened by the rum and the wine.

If Tate wasn't going to act like a captain, I didn't have to treat him as one, after all.

"You don't like being in private with me, lately," he teased. He laughed - taking any possible sting out of his words - and caught my fingers in his own, lifting my hand to his face and kissing my fingertips.

My breath caught in my chest and my cock instantly stood to attention as I gazed into his eyes.

"You really have no idea the effect you have on people, do you?" he murmured, tugging me closer to him by the hand. My wine sloshed over my other hand and I quickly took another drink to steady my nerves.

"I don't know what you mean," I muttered, mostly into the cup.

"I know you don't, that's what I'm saying." He chuckled, his eyes sparkling and kissed the back of my hand. I felt the soft brush of his moustache on my skin and my heart fluttered and warmth shot up my arm like prickly tingles, igniting my blood.

"Tate..."

His lips froze on my skin and he frowned, his eyes on the back of my hand or my coat cuff. Setting his rum down he tugged the cuff of my coat.

He was going to see the marks from the rope if I wasn't careful.

"Well, look at the time," I said, desperate suddenly to get out of his sight. Tate's grip tightened on my hand and he shoved the red satin sleeve of my coat up my arm, exposing the barely faded red marks from where Ezra had tied me up.

My blood thundered in my ears - fear, arousal and a desperate need to reassure Tate all warring with one another.

"What have you been doing?" he murmured. Then, surprising me all over again, he kissed the inside of my wrist where the red indentations were and I almost passed out from the softness of his lips on the irritated skin.

"Ezra," I breathed. Because, apparently, despite it all I couldn't lie to Tate. He had been my first, and I still thought him handsome, interesting and alluring. My heart and my body both wanted him.

"Of course. And you liked the pain, didn't you?" His voice was soft, barely above a whisper.

He opened his mouth and gently bit the skin on my wrist and I couldn't suppress the shudder it sent through me. I half turned towards the ship railings and the sea beyond, wishing to hide my quite plain arousal from the rest of the ship.

"I didn't..." I couldn't lie to him. "I did like it, I suppose I didn't mean to... with him," I said. But that wasn't quite the truth either. I looked sideways at Tate, who was smiling still. I couldn't understand that. "Aren't you jealous? Angry?"

"I suppose I ought to be," he murmured, tugging me closer to him, close enough that I could feel the warmth of his chest against my shoulder. He licked the spot on my wrist and my head felt light. "But I'm not, I'm just wondering if I ought to claim you myself, if you're... if you're done avoiding me, that is."

My resolve had long been lost in the wind off the Caribbean. I didn't want to avoid the Captain, not truly. He had shown me something wonderful, and he had been kind about it. But Ezra was also in my mind - and in my heart if I was honest with myself - and I wasn't sure how to reconcile the two. If I could, ever.

"I'm..." I said. Tate straightened up, letting his arm drop although he still had his fingers twined tightly through mine. He looked over my shoulder and his expression shifted.

"Ezra," he said. His voice had gone from gentle and alluring to wary.

If I could have died purely from embarrassment, I would have then.

Although both of us were fully dressed, it felt as if we had been caught naked, in the act. I half turned to see Ezra, cup in hand, eyebrows raised.

"What are you two doing?" He said, his voice low, rasping against my arousal and heightening it.

How can I be so attracted to the both of them? I should pull my hand away from Tate's, but I don't want to. I don't want to let go of him. But I don't want to upset Ezra. I can't choose!

"I... the Captain and I," I started, but I had no idea how to finish that sentence, and my head had begun to swim.

Ezra's arm snaked around my waist and he moved in close.

Although he could have tugged me bodily away from the Captain, he did not. My hand was still firmly in Tate's grasp, my shoulder pressed into his chest and between the both of them I felt deliciously trapped.

Both of them were larger and stronger than I was. They could do anything to me, and I wouldn't be able to stop them. The thought heated my blood even further, and my cock twitched. I hoped neither of them had noticed.

They eyed each other up, apparently ignoring the difficulty I was struggling with, or perhaps they were both just enjoying my plight.

"Perhaps, First Mate, this is a matter we should be discussing in private?" Tate suggested, amiably.

Beyond us, on the main deck, there were cheers and laughter - perhaps there had been sounds of the revels the entire time? It was hard to hear beyond the thundering of my own heart and the voices of the two men either side of me.

"If that's your wish, Captain," Ezra said. His voice held a stony edge to it and I shivered bodily.

"Lead the way to my cabin, Gideon," Tate said. The order cut through my arousal and confusion and I nodded. Both men let go of me, and one of them nudged me forward. I had no idea which.

My body felt suddenly cold, bereft, the places they'd been touching me no longer hot and fevered.

I cleared my throat, pulled my coat tighter around myself to cover my arousal and led the way to the Captain's cabin. I kept my eyes on the deck, unwilling to see if the crew observed this strange parade, for I could hear Tate and Ezra behind me and I was almost beside myself with excitement, fear and anticipation.

Were they about to fight over me?

Or were we all three about to...?

The wine and rum had removed my inhibitions and worries, and Tate had replaced it all with wild and intense desire. Ezra's appearing behind me had only heightened it all, and my mind was flooded with desire.

I don't want them to fight. As romantic as it might sound to have two men duelling over me like some romantic heroine, I don't want that. I don't want to ruin their professional relationship, to skewer their friendship.

I want us all to respect each other, and be amiable.

There's Captain Tate's bed, and I'm already aroused. With both these gorgeous attractive men behind me. I have to admit it.

I want them both.

But that could never happen, right?

CHAPTER SIXTEEN - IN WHICH IT COULD HAPPEN, ACTUALLY

*T*ate's cabin felt tiny. I went in first and stopped in the centre of the room, but then Tate and Ezra were in there with me and I was crowded back towards the bed. The door shut behind us.

"What is happening?" I asked. The swimmy feeling in my head had evaporated almost as soon as I realised I wanted the both of them, at the same time, and what that would entail. I felt sober and uncertain, but also undoubtedly heightened with anticipation.

"You really want to do this?" Tate asked, he was looking at Ezra, who shrugged a little.

"Please don't fight," I said, quickly.

"I wasn't suggesting a fight," Tate said. He reached for my hand and squeezed it. "If you're interested, and I suspect you are if I'm reading you right, I'm suggesting all three of us have sex."

My heart possibly stopped at that moment, because although it was a shockingly blunt and inappropriate thing to suggest, it was also definitely what I wanted. Maybe they had read my mind somehow?

"It wouldn't be my first time with more than one…" Ezra replied. My mind filled with salacious and attractive images of Ezra naked and with more than one partner. I had thought I was hard before, but now I felt much more aroused. Like I needed a release and fast, or things would get very painful.

"Gideon?" Tate asked. He put his hand on my shoulder and I didn't trust myself not to say something ridiculously lewd so instead I just nodded. I imagined my face would be conveying just how enthusiastic I was about the whole idea. Apparently I was unable to conceal any emotion, after all.

"Well, then," Ezra leaned back against the door and smirked at me. "Guess we'd all better get naked then."

I looked at Tate, my hands were shaking and I wasn't quite ready to just strip in front of both of them, so I moved towards him, and went to undo his waistcoat.

"That's it," Tate murmured, reassuring. His eyes were warm and he put a hand on my shoulder and squeezed. It gave me the courage to push the waistcoat open and undo the ties on his shirt, pushing my fingers against his skin and feeling the muscles below.

He tilted his chin down and I went up on my toes to meet him for a soft kiss. My eyes fluttered closed and I pressed closer to him.

I pulled his shirt off his shoulders and stroked my hands over his huge, hard chest. I felt the rumble of his approving groan under my fingers.

"Let's get this ridiculous thing off you." Ezra growled from behind me, and he took my coat off. I had to stop touching Tate to allow this, so I pulled back from the kiss and glanced over my shoulder. I felt a little stung.

"You think my coat's ridiculous?" It seemed easier to

concentrate on that than think too hard about what was about to happen. "It's my favourite."

"Aye, it's ridiculous, but it suits you, like a peacock parading his finery," Ezra said.

Although this should have been insulting, Ezra punctuated his words with soft kisses to my neck, under my ear. He lifted my hair with one hand and kissed the back of my neck.

Meanwhile Tate was unfastening my trousers. I didn't know what to do with my hands, so I reached up and behind my head with one, burying my hand in the dark mass of Ezra's hair, surprised at how soft it felt.

The other landed on Tate's bicep, where my thumb rubbed small circles. Tate slipped his hand inside my trousers and then I couldn't think about anything at all but physical sensations.

Ezra pressed close behind me, his hands shoving my trousers off my hips as he rubbed his own hardness against my rear. I groaned loudly.

That damn wanton harlot sound, I can't control it.

Tate surged forward to kiss me, harder this time, and Ezra spat into his hand. Then I felt his wet finger teasing at me.

I realised that the sounds I made had a benefit I hadn't foreseen. They didn't exist merely to humiliate me, but to encourage my lover. Lovers.

Both of them. Ezra and Tate, at the same time.

I kissed Tate back and moaned into his mouth. My hand slid up his arm and around to the back of his neck, holding him in the kiss as Ezra stretched me open again. The ache of it was delicious, and I suspected I was still somewhat ready from our encounter earlier.

I broke the kiss with Tate to try and catch my breath - which of course, proved impossible. Tate shifted some, I felt Ezra's chest press hard against my back and then they were kissing each other over my shoulder. One warm strong hand slowly pumping my cock and another teasing at my rear.

It was overwhelming. These two, huge and powerful men with me pressed in between them - trapped - my heart pounding and my breath so shallow I feared I might faint before the really good things happened.

"Oil?" Ezra growled so low I wasn't sure if I'd actually heard it or felt it through my bones.

Tate pulled back reluctantly and I whined as he moved away. Swiftly, as if he had been waiting for this moment, Ezra gripped me by my hips and turned me around. My trousers were around my knees and I almost toppled over, would have, if Ezra hadn't had such a firm grip on me.

I kicked the clothes away and shrugged off my open shirt. Ezra, still fully clothed, claimed my mouth then. His kiss again harder, more possessive than Tate's had been a moment before.

In a frenzy, I tore at his shirt lacings and shoved the clothing off his shoulders, thrilled that this time I was allowed to touch and explore his skin so freely.

Tate's hand touched my back and I broke the kiss to look over my shoulder at him.

"I'd like to..." The Captain blushed, which - given our current circumstances - I hadn't been aware he'd be capable of. He looked down and then at Ezra. "I'd like to fuck Gideon, unless either of you have an objection?"

I nodded and pushed my hips back encouraging him. He slicked a finger in the oil and took over from where Ezra had been teasing me.

My breath hitched as I looked up at Ezra, panting like a dog. His eyes were dark with lust, and I thought I saw a flicker of something like anger. Or maybe it was just his need to dominate and possess.

One of my hands teased at his nipple, and the other slipped down to undo his trousers. He helped me to remove them and I closed my hand on his cock with a relieved sigh.

"Gideon," he breathed. He wrapped an arm around my shoulders and tugged me towards the bed. I moved with him, but slowly, not wanting to lose Tate's finger. Tate wrapped his arm around my waist and together they lifted me to the bed.

Almost sobbing with need, I went to my hands and knees, pushing my rear up towards Tate. Ezra knelt before me and buried a hand in my hair, tugging my mouth down to his cock.

"Lick me, pet," he murmured.

I opened my mouth and licked the length of him, groaning at the salty taste and smiling at his responding shudder. This was something new, and I liked it.

Behind me I heard Tate grunt. "Pet?"

"Oh yes," Ezra said. "This little whore is my pet. You could be too if you like?"

I closed my eyes, intent on my job of licking at Ezra, but imagining what Tate might look like, tied up or in chains. Mine to do what I liked with, or both of us at Ezra's mercy. My cock jolted and I felt it leaking.

Good Lord, but I want that, I want all of that. I want to try absolutely everything with both of them. I want to feel everything I am capable of feeling.

I didn't hear Tate's reply, instead I felt his cock pressing against me. It was larger again than Ezra's and I felt my body stretch around him, accommodating him. My breath caught and I paused from licking at Ezra as I tried to breathe, feeling myself adjust.

"Please," I managed to moan, my voice cracked and strained.

"Please, what, love?" Tate asked, I felt his hand stroke a warm line over my spine. Reassuring, kind and gentle.

He stopped moving and I whined, because that was the absolute opposite of what I wanted.

I shoved my hips back, trying to impale myself on him. "More," I croaked and he stroked my back again, his other hand on my hip as he eased himself inside. That delicious pull and slide that made my cock ache with need.

Ezra's hand tightened in my hair and he pulled me back against him. Eagerly, I opened my mouth and took the tip of him inside, rolling my tongue around him, careful not to scrape too hard with my teeth.

I couldn't stop moaning, which made the act of sucking on Ezra a little difficult. Tate inside me further complicated matters, and I had to force myself to concentrate on my job, pushing my tongue against the shaft again and again.

Tate pulled his hips back and then shoved them forward again, his cock filling me deliciously.

"Fucking hell," Ezra moaned. "You're a natural at that, pet." He tugged on my hair, easing my head back and forth gently as I licked at him. "Keep going."

I felt Tate press harder against my ass and then the sounds of them kissing over my back.

If only there were a way to participate and watch it all as well, I thought wildly. *They must look so hot kissing, both of them inside me in some way. I wish I could see it. I wish I could...*

I moved my hand to stroke myself, desperate for a little relief.

The pressure from Tate eased and I heard him chuckle. "Are we neglecting you, love?" He thrust harder and I moaned around Ezra's cock.

"Not without permission," Ezra said. His hand closed around my arm and pulled it behind my back and I whined noisy, wanting so much.

If I had been at liberty to speak, I would have let loose a stream of every swear word I knew. Instead I swallowed around Ezra's cock, determined to bring him off and somehow earn my own pleasure.

Ezra gasped and his hips surged up, filling my mouth and shoving at the back of my throat so that I choked on him. Blinking away tears, I repeated the movement, taking him as deep as I could as he groaned. I didn't choke the second time, my throat seemed to anticipate the movement and I shoved my tongue against him as hard as I could in the same moment.

I felt his cock pulse and his seed filled my mouth. Above me, he cried out, his grip on my arm tightening so I moaned again, all the while swallowing as much of it as I could manage.

He pulled out of my mouth and I swallowed again, licking my lips clean and panting hard, my head sinking onto the bed between his thighs.

Tate's hips moved faster now, his hand on my hip holding me still so he could pull himself out almost the whole way and then slam deep inside me again. Tate's hand found my cock and pumped it as well.

I was beyond words, panting and hot, revelling in the sensation of him using me - my body - to get himself to completion.

Ezra's hand remained in my hair but now it was stroking gently, but his other hand still gripped my arm, holding it uncomfortably behind my back. In a way I was glad of it, as it showed I still was his, despite Tate fucking me so hard I was being driven into the bed, my cheek mashed against the bedclothes. With one eye cracked open I could see Tate above me, his mouth slack and his eyes half closed.

"Ready? Come on, come with me," Tate gasped. Ezra leaned over me to kiss his neck and shoulders.

Tate's hand squeezed me and I came with a strained noise of pleasure, something like a moan and a scream as the release washed over me.

I felt I had left the room, I was somewhere up in the sky, caressed by angels. It was a heady sensation, and in some ways I felt a strange kind of potential in it. Something promised by the cosmos, perhaps, but I had no way to understand it.

Tate, urged on by my squeezing of him, bucked against me once more and I felt his warm seed fill me.

Coming back to myself with a jolt, I melted into the bed, feeling utterly boneless and satisfied. Tate withdrew and I felt a soft, damp cloth clean me up.

Ezra let go of my arm finally and they both stroked my limbs and lifted me up to lay between them on the bed. All three of us panting hard, our limbs tangled together.

CHAPTER SEVENTEEN - IN WHICH THE WEATHER CHANGES AND SOMETHING IS LOST

After a few minutes I came back to most of my senses. Tate had his arm around my shoulders, and Ezra's head rested on his wrist. My right leg was draped over Ezra's thighs, and I had a hand on each of their waists.

"That was something," Tate said, somewhat dreamily.

"A very good something," Ezra murmured. He sounded half asleep. His hand found my wrist and he held it lightly - his version of holding hands perhaps?

"What did you think, Gideon?" Tate shifted a little, his hand closing over mine.

"Why is your name Gideon and not Aaron?" Ezra asked.

"Oh hush, now's not the time for that," Tate said. "Let the boy recover before he tells us all his secrets."

"I liked it," I mumbled. I probably should come clean with them both about my true identity, now that we had shared something so intimate, all three of us. But my head felt full of fog still.

Ezra half turned and stroked my hair back from my

shoulder. "Yeah? I liked it too," he said. Leaning in he kissed my shoulder.

"Me too," Tate said. He stretched mightily, and I felt all his muscles tense and relax against my side and under my head. "We should probably do it again. This time I want Ezra to fuck me while Gideon rides my face."

I shivered and my breath hitched for what felt like the thousandth time that day.

"Maybe give him a moment to recover," Ezra said. He suppressed a laugh.

Tate laughed heartily and my head bobbed up and down on his bicep from the movement, causing me to laugh as well. "Aye, maybe in an hour or so?"

There was a shout from out on deck and then the ship's bell started to ring. Not just once or twice for the watch, but continuously, insistently.

Tate sat up abruptly. I rolled away so he wouldn't squash me and found myself pressed against Ezra, our noses practically touching. He stole a kiss and gave me a wink.

"Better check that out." Tate hurriedly pulled on his trousers.

Ezra kissed me again and Tate leaned over to smack him smartly on the rear, causing him to jolt against me. "You too, Ezra, could be trouble."

Ezra, grumbling, rolled off the bed and looked around for his own trousers.

I caught sight of his tattoo again. More than simply being a beautiful piece of art on a beautiful man, it tugged at something at my memory.

The bell sounded louder and I scrambled out of bed.

I pulled on my trousers, not wanting to stay alone and naked in the Captain's cabin.

Tate shoved the door open and swore. Although the sun had barely dropped towards the horizon, the sky was dark with gathering clouds.

"Storm," Ezra breathed, and pulled his jacket back on. I cast around for my red coat and slipped it on before hurrying out to help in any way I could.

Storms are bad news, I thought wildly. My heart was instantly pounding at the sound of the word, remembering that terrible storm from my time in the Navy. *I won't be up the mast this time, though.*

The crew were busy sealing barrels and rolling them below deck, securing sails and battening down the hatches.

For a moment I hesitated on the deck, unsure how I could best help and what I could do without being in the way.

Above me were men in the riggings, and my breath caught in fear, terrified for them.

They're so high up, what if they get stuck? Worse, what if they fall to the deck? It would surely kill them.

Tate was barking orders to the crew, Ezra had taken the helm, hauling it around so the bow of the ship was pointed into the waves.

Shaking my head to try and clear it of fear and unwanted memories, I went to help Shem to tie the mainsail down, hauling on the sheets and helping to knot them.

The ocean was rapidly becoming rough as the wind picked up, bringing with it heavy rain and a strange sort of sound.

"What is that?" I asked, but the wind tore my words away unheard.

The rain was chill and soaked through my coat and pants instantly, making my teeth chatter.

"Get down!" There was a hand on my shoulder, I turned to

see Joseph shouting over the gale. "Get below deck or tie yourself to the mast!"

"Right," I said. Then I nodded, so he'd know I understood him because there was no way he'd hear me over the gale.

This was easier said than done. The waves had become so large the deck was rocking below my bare feet.

The gale shoved me sideways when I let go of the mast. I dug my toes into the deck as much as I could and made my way towards the stairway.

Then I remembered Zeb - he was in my cabin. Would he be safe in there? He'd surely be afraid.

"Get below! To the bunks!" Tate bellowed, his voice carrying over the wind. But that strange sound as well, I heard it again. There was another voice in the wind.

A voice in the wind could mean only one thing.

"A witch," I breathed. This storm was no ordinary bit of weather.

I grabbed onto the railings on the side of the ship as a large wave tipped us to the starboard side. I clung on as the ship righted itself. Shivering with cold and fear, I pulled myself along the side of the ship. There - my cabin - I was close.

The wind howled higher, the shrill voice inside it seeming to scream now. It tore at my hair and coat, tugging at me. I grabbed the closest piece of rope and wound it around my arm.

I should've stayed in Tate's cabin, then I'd be safe.

But Zeb! I have to make sure he's safe, too.

I wish Tate was holding me safe and tight.

I focused my gaze on my cabin door. It wasn't so far, just ten steps. I could do this. I unwound myself from the rope and swallowed. My entire body was chilled from the cold and the wind. I wanted to wrap my arms around myself to stay warm, but I needed them spread out to the side for balance.

I looked up to see Ezra clinging to the helm with grim determination, looking every inch the brooding hero of one of my penny romance novels.

I love him, I thought. Then I turned to see Tate, striding towards me, shirtless and impressive. *I love him, too.*

"Get down, you idiot!" He roared.

I hurried a couple of steps towards my cabin door. It was nearly within reach.

Then the deck under my feet lurched downwards and an almighty wave crashed over the deck. Over me.

My feet skidded over the wooden boards.

I couldn't breathe.

I tasted salt.

Knocked down and sideways, I was now scrabbling at the boards with my fingers, sliding down towards the ocean.

Pain in my leg. An impact. I'd hit the side of the ship.

Then I was in the water, flailing, trying to swim up but which way was up?

My lungs were on fire, desperate for air.

I flailed, hands finding nothing but more water.

I inhaled sea water.

My mind went dark.

CHAPTER EIGHTEEN - IN WHICH GIDEON LEARNS SOME THINGS ABOUT THE PAST

I woke coughing up water.

I vomited out as much as I could onto the stone floor I rested on and coughed pathetically from the salt abrading my throat.

My whole body hurt in a myriad of different ways. My eyes were blurred and thick with salt, too.

I felt scrambled, woken from a deep and unknowable dream.

"Ah, you're awake then," a voice said.

Do I know that voice? No. No that's a new voice.

I blinked, coughed up another mouthful of water and spat on the ground. I looked around.

I swiped my arm across my eyes to clear them. I was in a cave, the floor a wave smoothed rock. Behind me was a pool, a cave entrance, the sea beyond. In front of me stood a man.

Instantly I recognised him as a witch. His skin was pale, with a grey pallor. His eyes were large and deep. There was a beading or scaling, something shiny on the skin of his temples, seeming to spread down beside his eyes and onto his cheekbones. Maybe fish scales? Maybe pearls and crystal rocks embedded in his skin?

He stood tall and lean, a ragged black cloak hung from his shoulders. His chest bare, and a pair of worn trousers his only other clothing.

I'm done for. This is surely Solomon.

Solomon who hates Tate and probably meant to get Tate instead of me. Tate was close to me... I hope the wave didn't catch him, too. I hope he's safe.

He smiled at me, and I was surprised at the warmth in it. His teeth were white and even, and when he smiled, there was a dimple in his cheek.

"Solomon?"

He inclined his head. "Welcome to the Splintered Isles. Who, exactly, are you?"

I coughed, trying to ease the wretched scratchiness of my throat and pushed myself up into a kneeling position. My legs felt sore and I didn't trust myself to stand without falling down.

"Gideon... Gideon Keene," I said. I remembered too late I was trying to pretend I was someone else.

Well, I'd almost drowned. And now I was in a cave with a murderous sea witch. Chances were I was about to die. A false name seemed pointless now.

"Gideon Keene..." The man said, as if tasting the name on his tongue. "Keene is a familiar name. Who is your father?"

"My father?" I breathed. "My father is Governor of Kingston, Jamaica."

I probably shouldn't have told him that, but something about him drew the truth out of me.

A spell, I realised. He had a truth spell of some sort on me.

I let my head drop and tried to think of some way to escape,

BargainBookStores.com

Name: Rosalind Perry
E-mail: 0d29ec28689f3902f126@membe
rs.ebay.com

Order Date: 1/4/2021 3:27:14 AM

Ship Method: US_DGMSmartMailGround

Order #: 0179782OE1
PO #: PO-21073121-IBC

Seller Order: 09-06347-21700

Qty	ISBN/UPC	Title	Price
1		Cabin Boy: A gay harem paranormal romance (Paperback or Softback)	$13.23

Questions:

Subtotal:	$13.23
Shipping:	$0.00
Tax:	$0.99
Total:	$14.22

0179782OE1

TO REORDER YOUR UPS DIRECT THERMAL LABELS:

1. Access our supply ordering website at **UPS.COM**®
   or contact UPS at 800-877-8652

2. Please refer to Label # 01774006 when ordering.

01774006   RRD

but with a witch in front of me and the sea behind me it seemed utterly hopeless. I'd even lost my red coat, and was cowering on the ground in nothing but my waterlogged trousers.

"Governor Keene, of course…. And he has ships out looking for you." He crouched in front of me.

His fingers touched me under my chin and tipped my head up, forcing me to look him in the eyes. His eyes were a deep blue black. The sea at night.

Oh God, he's stealing my soul, isn't he? He's got me here, under a truth spell, and now he's going to suck the soul right out of my body.

"He does?" I asked. My voice still raspy and hoarse.

"You weren't aware? All the trade winds are abuzz with your name. Gideon Keene, stolen away by pirates. Your father has offered quite the reward for your return, and the capture or death of the pirates. I mean, obviously there were already bounties on them. Especially that first mate, the one with the shearwater tattoo."

My memory stirred and I realised why I had thought I recognised something about Ezra's beautiful bird tattoo. Father had a vendetta against the Shearwater tattooed pirate. He'd sworn he would see him hanged on several occasions.

How had I not realised this before?

"Of course it would all come together like this," Solomon continues. "Tate stole you from your father, and now I've stolen you from him."

"He didn't steal me," I said, a stubborn loyalty to Tate surging up in my chest. "I ran away."

"Ah." His fingers dug harder into the soft flesh under my chin, forcing me to kneel up straighter, look up at him. "You ran away? Why would you do such a thing?"

The truth pulled at me and I couldn't stop the words flowing out of my mouth like sea water. "I didn't want to marry a girl. I like boys, I like... sex with men," I said. I was sure, if I wasn't still chilled to the bone, I would be blushing.

"Do you now?" Solomon smiled wider. "Stand up, Gideon. Let me look at you."

I stood, uncertain if he had compelled me or if I had simply wanted to stand. My legs shook, weak and bruised. I wrapped my arms around myself and shivered.

"Ah, cold are you?" He lifted his arm in a quick flicking gesture and a warm wind blew from deep inside the cave, flowing over me and heating my body.

"Th-thank you?" I said hesitantly. It seemed strange that he would take care of me in such a manner. A wicked sea witch who was concerned I was cold? Something wasn't adding up.

He walked slowly around me, his eyes moving up and down my body, examining me from every angle.

"How long have you been on the ship?" he asked, from behind me, circling again like a shark.

"The Grey Kelpie?"

Solomon moved in front of me and nodded, although I saw one of his eyes twitch with annoyance.

I tried to think. How long had it been? A week? No, longer than that. Ten days? Two weeks? Assuming I'd only been unconscious for a couple of hours...

"Two weeks or so, maybe a few days more," I said.

Solomon stopped in front of me, his eyebrows raised. "Really? Just two weeks and you're the most precious cargo on the ship?"

"Most... precious?" My heart thumped hard and I shook my head. My hair, still damp, plastered itself across my cheek so I pulled it back with one hand and twisted it together. "I don't know what you mean by that."

"It doesn't matter, you must be very talented, or special, is all it means." Quick as a flash of lightning his hand flashed out and closed around my wrist.

He let go again, but I could still feel his hand there. Looking down there was a thin silver chain wrapped around my wrist where his hand had been. It sealed itself closed and led to his hand with a tethering chain.

My heart sank.

So I'm a prisoner here. Well, at least he hasn't killed me outright, I suppose.

Solomon turned and walked deeper into the cave, the chain pulling taut between us before I reluctantly followed him. What was I going to do? Make him drag me?

Chain this time. Same wrist that had the rope marks on it that Tate was kissing.

I flushed and swallowed the sudden arousal. *This is not the time.*

Couldn't I even be a prisoner of an evil sea witch without being plagued with salacious thoughts? It was like the moment I left my Father's house, my libido had taken over my entire body.

I tried to put such thoughts out of my head and follow Solomon. The path he led along had a bit of an incline up and was softly lit by unseen - likely magical - sources. The caves were narrow, but not too low ceilinged. Solomon appeared to have a good few inches on me, but imagining him next to Tate he would have been the shorter one.

Soon we came to a staircase and he climbed it, tugging me along behind him. He remained silent so I did too, unwilling to spill any more truths than I already had to him.

As we climbed the stairs my knees began to ache, my thigh hurt from where I'd collided with the ship when the wave had taken me. I was out of breath when we reached the top of the stairs, feeling weak and battered.

The staircase opened into what had to be Solomon's home, or part of it at least.

The stairway had curled around the walls of a vertical passage at the back of a system of caves. This part was a wide, flat cave looking out on a spectacular view of the ocean.

We must be someway up a mountain, to get such a vista.

The cave walls had several tunnels and smaller caves leading off it, like a terraced house made of a cave. The main room, if that was where we were, had a stone bench set out as if you might sit and appreciate the view. The cave wall had recessed shelves and there was a Persian rug on the floor.

It was quite bright outside, the sun must be nearing midday, and although I drank in the sight of the sunshine it hurt my eyes after the dim caves.

Assuming it's the next day, I've been unconscious all night and most of the morning. How did I get from the ship to the cave? What magic bore me here? It can't have been Solomon himself...

But perhaps I do not want to know the answer to that.

Instead, I looked around the large room. There was a tug on my arm and Solomon led me into one of the side caves. It appeared to be a living space - mismatched blankets and cushions were scattered over a large wooden framed bed with a mattress, a chaise to one side made of a totally different wood sat on a Persian rug of rich greens and golds. There were more rugs and tapestries hung on the stone wall and soft golden lights radiated from spots on the wall.

"How did you find this place?" I asked, despite myself, I was in awe, and I felt a certain amount of desire to praise the abode I was a guest in. Damn etiquette lessons again.

I don't think preparatory school etiquette extends to being the prisoner of a sea witch.

"I formed it out of the rocks," Solomon said.

"But the furnishings," I started.

"Shipwrecks provide most of my things." He smirked unpleasantly and led me to the chaise. "Put your wrists together."

I did so without hesitation. I had no desire at all to anger him, for although he was speaking to me in a civilised manner, he could still kill me at any time. I needed to know his motivations, and his intentions before I could plan an escape.

He looped the chain around both my wrists, and I watched, fascinated as the chain sealed itself securely around me. He tugged a length free and wrapped it around the leg of the chaise.

"There, you can sit, stand or lay down." He said, letting go as the chain sealed itself.

Imagine if Ezra had a chain like this...

"You caused the storm yesterday," I blurted - anything to keep my mind off the memories of Ezra and what being bound by the wrists had meant with him.

"Indeed," he said. He ran both hands through his hair and yawned. "Tate sailed close enough I could smell the bastard."

I frowned, something didn't add up. I sat on the chaise, my right leg was throbbing now and I rubbed it gently with my hand.

"Tate sails close, but not too close," I said. "He said we'd keep a safe distance."

"Ah." Solomon said. "But was Tate at the helm when the

storm hit you?" He smirked, giving me a knowing look and I had to look away as my cheeks flamed.

"No, he was not."

"Mm." Solomon busied himself at a desk I hadn't noticed before. It was recessed some from the main room, in a small cave. The recess was lined with jars of specimens and liquids, bundles of dried herbs and seaweeds, and I spied a stack of books in the corner of the table as well. I itched to pick them up and read the titles. Somehow I didn't think that would be allowed.

"And what was he doing instead?" Solomon asked, idly.

I could feel the truth pushing at my tongue, bubbling up in my throat, but I clenched my teeth shut. Whatever the history between the two of them, telling him of the relationship between Tate and I would likely be hazardous - if he knew Tate cared about me, what would he do?

The silence stretched out.

Solomon turned back to me, his cloak swirled around him with the suddenness of the movement.

"You're resisting? Impressive... I wonder how it is you can resist at all."

I ground my teeth together so hard they hurt.

Solomon approached and with a gentle hand caressed my jaw. It was so warm, so soft a touch that I leaned into it without thinking.

"You're really very interesting, aren't you? There's something about you. Obviously you're attractive, and there's a vulnerability about you that's enticing. But there's something more, yes, there's something else at work inside you." He leaned in, gazing into my eyes with an intensity I almost couldn't bear, but I held his gaze.

I might be a prisoner here, but I wouldn't say anything that would betray Tate, Ezra or the Grey Kelpie.

I felt words in my throat, tickling at my tongue, but I kept my mouth shut. He stroked his hand down my jaw and throat and prodded his finger into the old bruise Ezra had left.

"A strength to you, but not one you're aware of perhaps," Solomon mused. "Fascinating. You know…" he let go of me and moved away again. "You speak a lot without words."

"I speak - what?" I blurted before I could stop myself.

"Your expressions, your body language, it's all rather easy to read I'm afraid." He smiled wide. "And besides, my spell was quite specific on what I wanted from the Grey Kelpie."

A chill ran up my spine.

Had he really been able to read me? And what was that spell? And whatever had he meant about me having a strength I wasn't aware of? So many questions.

"Specific about what you wanted…?" I mumbled, then smothered my own mouth with both my bound hands.

"Aye, I cast the storm, and sent spirits with it. The spirits were to identify the thing most valuable on the ship. Whatever it was that Tate cared the most about, his most precious cargo, and bring that to me."

I shivered bodily, although terrified all over again, some small part of me thrilled that I could be the thing that Tate most prized.

But of course, that meant Solomon had what he wanted, and… Tate would come to the Isles to rescue me? To get me back? Surely he wouldn't be so stupid. But then, if he really cared that much?

"There, now, you understand." Solomon said. "Are you hungry?"

I wanted very much to say no, but my stomach rumbled noisily. I hated my body for still wanting food, and hungering for other things, while I was in such danger.

"I see. Take a rest if you like, you're quite safe for the moment. I'll prepare something cooked for you."

He left the room and I sat on the chaise, looking around me.

There were several worrying things in his statements. The fact he could read me even if I didn't speak. He'd also said 'safe for now', which implied things I didn't wish to think about. Besides that there was the whole 'precious to Tate' thing, which needed some pondering.

I hoped that Tate didn't take the bait and come to stage a rescue, as Solomon would surely have set up a trap.

But I also desperately wished to be rescued. Although Solomon hadn't exactly mistreated me, I didn't trust him at all. There was no real upside to being his prisoner and if I could get away maybe Tate wouldn't have to risk himself getting to me.

Alone in the room, I tried to slip my hands out from the chains, but they were fastened tight enough I couldn't get my hands through the loops. Leaning down, I tugged on the chain where it circled around the chaise leg. It didn't budge.

My head swam, and my vision went muzzy.

I shouldn't have leaned my head down so far.

Giving up, I groaned and collapsed onto the chaise, letting my poor head rest on the soft cushion.

My eyes slipped closed. Maybe I could sleep a little. Let oblivion take me.

What on Earth was going to happen to me next?

CHAPTER NINETEEN - IN WHICH THE GREY KELPIE IS ALMOST HIT BY LIGHTNING

Tate had watched as the wave had taken Gideon.

There had been no doubt that wave had been sent by Solomon. It had swept up in the ocean like a whale, looking for something. It had crashed deliberately onto Gideon - and only Gideon - and sucked him overboard. No other wave had done any such thing, and as soon as Gideon was off the boat, the wind picked up, threatening to tear the sails loose. A boom of thunder overhead startled everyone still on the upper decks.

Lightning struck the sea beside the ship soon after, and another deafening boom thundered over them.

Tate strode across the deck to grasp the rails where Gideon had gone overboard. There was no sign of him. Lost. He had to assume he was lost or taken. Uncertain of which Solomon would prefer.

He shook his head, he had a ship to save, and plenty of souls left on board. He couldn't let himself get distracted or everyone would be drowned.

He made his way to the helm where Ezra was braced, a rope holding him to the wheel in case of another wave.

"Solomon," Tate said. "He's taken Gideon."

Ezra nodded. The wind no longer had a voice in it, which was something, but Solomon clearly wasn't done with them. The thunder and lightning remained close over the ship, and Tate feared that lightning would strike the mast, set the ship alight.

If that happened, well, they were all lost.

A faint hope in his chest told him that if Solomon meant to drown them all he wouldn't have carefully stolen Gideon first.

He put a hand on Ezra's shoulder and leaned close enough to speak into his ear. "How far are we from the Splintered Isles?"

"I don't know." Ezra turned his face, so close to Tate's he could kiss him again if either of them had been in the mood for it. "With this rain, visibility is shot, for all I know we're close to dashing ourselves on the rocks. Or we might be miles out."

"We're close enough for his spells," Tate replied.

He squeezed Ezra's shoulder, wanting to give him some reassurance. Ezra nodded, let go of the wheel with one hand long enough to awkwardly pat Tate on the shoulder.

Tate hurried to his cabin, almost slipping on the slick deck once, before pulling himself up to his full height.

"I'm captain of this bloody cursed ship," he muttered into the wind. "And I'll not give up, and I'll not fall down."

He considered addressing Solomon directly, letting the rain carry his curses and anger directly to the sea witch's ears, but there didn't seem to be much wisdom in baiting him further. Tate was smart enough to know he had the weaker position, just surviving would be the challenge for the moment.

In his cabin, he snatched up his spyglass and pulled a heavy woollen coat over his shoulders. He secured the door on the way out and made his way to the bow, waiting for the next lightning strike to light the night up so he could look around.

It took several minutes, several lightning strikes, before he made out the murky shape of the mountains on the Isles. Turning, he gestured to Ezra. They were a safe distance off the rocks, and although some part of him was considering urging the ship forwards to the island, finding Gideon and getting him back, the larger, more logical part knew they had no chance in this storm.

His heart yearned to retrieve his lover though. He allowed himself a moment to think of Gideon, that strange young man they'd picked up who wasn't who he said he was. He seemed to be weaving a spell all of his own over himself and Ezra, possibly other members of the crew too... he tamped down on the desire to pursue immediately. It was more than foolishness, it was suicide.

He had to survive the storm to have any chance of finding out Gideon's fate.

Whether Solomon wanted to kill them all or not, if they sailed too close to the rocks and coral that skirted the islands they'd be lost, they couldn't risk that.

They had to ride the storm out first.

If they could.

He rejoined Ezra at the helm.

CHAPTER TWENTY - IN WHICH
GIDEON TALKS WITH A WITCH

J woke warm and comfortable. My bed on the ship is
so good... or was I in Captain Tate's bed? I smiled to
myself and went to turn over, looking for Tate. Then I realised
my hands were bound and I thought *Ezra* and opened my eyes,
eager and flushed with sudden excitement.

No.

Solomon's inner sanctum. I was curled on my side on the
chaise and a warm blanket had been placed over me. The room
was filled with a delicious smell. Hot food. My stomach rumbled
again.

I shifted. The thoughts of Tate and Ezra had me a somewhat
aroused, and I wanted to quell that before Solomon came in.

*Just think, you're in mortal peril. That's not sensual. Mortal peril
is terrifying and serious business.*

My body took a little more convincing. I sat up, sniffing the
air, the blanket slipped off my shoulders and I struggled to get it
back up over me but the chains were too tight.

I sighed some, shivered once, although it wasn't actually that
cold in the cave.

I cleared my throat. The smell was really getting to me. I was salivating, and my stomach rumbled loudly.

"Uh, hello?" I called to the room. My voice echoed through the cave and then reverberated back at me.

Surely, Solomon had heard, wherever he was. He must have a kitchen somewhere in this cave system. How strange to think of him here, carving a house out of the side of a mountain. Making it comfortable. Stealing things from shipwrecks to furnish and decorate it.

I heard the sound of footsteps and hurriedly pulled the blanket over my lap. My damn cock was still somewhat hard and I didn't want him to see.

The sea witch rounded the corner carrying a tray with a cover over it. He set it down on a small table near the chaise.

"Sleep well, did you?" Solomon asked mildly.

"Well enough," I said. My attention was largely on the tray and the smells wafting off it.

Solomon reached for my lap and for a crazed moment I thought he was going to tug the blanket aside and stroke my hardness. Instead he wrapped a hand around the chain on my wrists and pulled it free.

"Leg."

"Leg?" I blinked up at him, uncomprehending.

"Stick your leg out for me," he said, irritably.

"Oh right." I tucked the blanket over my lap and stuck out my leg.

With a quick movement and what I think was a wink, he looped the chain around my ankle.

"There, now you can easily eat. I don't know how much of a fighter you are, but know that if you try anything I can put you back to sleep in an instant. If you anger me, things will not go easily for you. I've been kind so far, but I don't have to be."

He raised an eyebrow, examining my face.

I was sure I'd gone paler still, and I nodded. He didn't actually have to say any of that, although I had thought of escape, I knew I was outclassed by him if it came to a fight.

"I wouldn't dare," I said, earnestly. He nodded, apparently seeing the truth in my words.

"Then enjoy your lunch." He shifted the table holding the tray closer to me and I lifted the cover to reveal half a smoked fish, a steaming bread roll and a heap of greens beside it.

My stomach made an insistent noise.

What if it's poison? A small voice in the back of my head asked. But I put that idea aside. I'd been unconscious around Solomon more than I'd been awake. If his plan was to kill me he'd had ample opportunity and hadn't taken it.

I fell upon the food hungrily and was gratified to find it was delicious and fresh.

"Thank you," I said between mouthfuls. "This is really good."

More politeness in the face of disaster and peril. Ah well, perhaps Mother would be proud of me for remaining civil instead of just crying and giving up?

"You're welcome," Solomon said lightly. He had moved back to his desk and was looking at something laid out on it.

He was polite as well, and well spoken, almost like a scholar. I wonder what his life had been like before he met Tate. Could a witch attend a school?

I ate a few more bites and then considered him, the lithe form under the long cloak, the curve of his neck as he half bent over his desk. He was very attractive, scary without a doubt, but fine of feature.

I found butter in a lump under one of the green leaves and spread it on the roll.

"What is your history with Tate?" I asked, finally.

I watched as every soft curve of Solomon became a sharp edge. I stopped chewing the bread and held my breath, wondering if now was when he'd show his truly cruel side to me, and what that would mean or what it would look like.

He pulled himself up to his full height and moved across the room, graceful as any ballet dancer. "What do you think it is?" he asked.

I inhaled, watching him closely as he pulled a chair over and sat down on it. I felt like one of the mice on the ship when Zebulon had sighted them.

"I'm not sure," I said, slowly, carefully. "Tate doesn't speak of you, and the crew have theories but... no one knows."

"Theories? So he doesn't speak of me but they know about me all the same?" He seemed amused by this, smiling and tapping his finger on his chin.

I got the feeling that he wasn't about to answer my question so I finished off the bread roll.

"Sagor-" I bit back on the full name. There was some lore that said a witch could do something with your full name. Solomon already had my full name, but I could try and protect the rest of the crew. "There are stories told of you on board," I finished.

"What kind of stories, tell me," he said. He sat back in his chair and settled comfortably. "I want to hear how I'm described on my old ship."

So that part was true, was it? He had been on the Grey Kelpie in the past. Even thought of it as his ship, as if he had some emotional attachment to it. I certainly wouldn't think of the Naval ship I was assigned to as 'my ship'. In fact, I had actively tried to forget the name of it.

I recounted what I could remember of what Sagorika had said, trying to make Solomon sound a little less evil.

Once I finished I ate a little more food as Solomon seemed to mull the stories over, pensively looking towards the wall.

"So, are they uh, accurate, any of them?" I asked. Somehow while I spoke Solomon had produced a bottle of wine and two cups, and he handed me one of them. "Thank you, so kind," I said absently.

"I'm not kind," Solomon snapped. I sat back on the chaise and cleared my throat. "There's a little truth in some of them."

I was silent for a moment, unsure about what to say next. He'd snapped at me, and then answered my question. He was sitting there, drinking wine with me as if we were, I don't know, friends?

Maybe he's lonely. There's no evidence that there's anyone else on this island, or at least in the immediate vicinity.

Why would he be sitting with me if he didn't want to talk?

"You can tell me, if you like," I said, quietly. "It's not like uh, I'm going to go and blab your secrets to anyone. Since, you know." I jiggled my leg so that the chain tinkled. "If you want to, I don't know, get it off your chest."

Solomon leaned his elbow on the arm of his chair, propped his chin on his hand and looked at me with raised eyebrows.

"Get it off my chest?" He repeated, incredulously.

"Well, sometimes it can help," I said. I sipped the wine and set it down, I felt rather like wine had led to this whole mess somehow. "On the ship there's this cat, uh, Zebulon. Zeb, and he comes into my cabin at night I tell him the things I've been worrying about, or the things I'm not sure of. You know, just talk it through out loud. It helps me sort through my thoughts, understand what I'm feeling. Somewhat."

I dropped my eyes, his gaze was very intense.

"Mm," Solomon said. He tapped his foot a few times, then got up and left the room.

Ah well, at least I tried.

CHAPTER TWENTY-ONE - IN WHICH GIDEON ATTEMPTS TO COMMUNICATE EMOTIONS

a few hours later, when I had tried every possible position of rest on and around my chaise, tested how far I could move away from it, and tried to reach something interesting and failed, the sea witch returned.

His hair was wild, standing up all over his head, his eyes were wide, and the hem of his cloak was stained with salt.

I sat up as he came back in and folded my hands in my lap, uncertain what was about to happen, but years of politeness kicking into my muscle memory.

"Fine," he said. He sat down on the chair again. "It has been a long time since I had someone human to talk to."

"Human?" I asked, without thinking.

Oh, I hope I didn't just put him off the whole idea of talking to me by butting in with a question.

"These islands are magical," Solomon said. "There are magical creatures here. Merfolk, talking birds, selkies and the like. Many of them... do not seek out my company."

I bit my lip so that I wouldn't comment on the possible reasons why that might be. I nodded encouragingly.

"The fact is, it's... well, it's lonely here," he said, and leaned back in the chair. "I spend most of my days reading or walking, and all the time thinking of that cursed man and his bloody cursed ship."

I inhaled through my nose and nodded. "You love him?"

"I hate him," he snapped. I flinched at the ferocity in his words.

"Right, sorry," I said.

"Once upon a time, maybe," he said, his voice softening. He looked past me, his eyes going cloudy as if a mist had dropped over them from within. "Things were different then, I was different. I hadn't come into my full power and I... he was different, too. Less mercenary."

It was hard to imagine Tate as mercenary. I had seen him so tender and so kind, but I'd perhaps seen a flash or two of how serious he could be. The last time I'd seen him - on the ship - he'd looked as if he could tear the deck apart with his bare hands. Standing shirtless in the middle of a storm.

Not the time to get aroused, you foolish idiot, I told myself sternly.

"It must've been a fun time for you both," I ventured.

He pulled his gaze back to my face and tilted his head to one side. "I suppose it was. Beyond the anger it's hard to remember other emotions."

"But they must have been there. There must have been some reason the two of you sailed together," I said, feeling bolder. He hadn't cursed me or struck me or anything yet. The conversation was going excellently, as far as I could tell.

"Certainly." He closed his eyes and a soft smile played over his face, quickly replaced by the melancholy he'd been displaying most of the time. "I never expected such a betrayal, so it hurt even more when it occurred."

"You don't have to tell me the details if you don't want to," I said. Some part of me was afraid to hear it, much as I loved Tate, I didn't want to hear about the darker side of him. "But it will surely do you good to consider your feelings about it."

His shoulders raised and fell and he sighed airily. "My feelings are all I ever think of, how angry I am, how hurt by his betrayal. We had a deal, you see, and before I knew it, I was cast aside. Literally, he left me here on these islands."

"You've been stranded here ever since?" A chill passed through me. How could the Tate I know do a thing like that? It was horrifying.

"Five years," he said, nodding. "I could have... perhaps... found my way off the islands. There have been other ships, and my magic has only grown. But I like it well enough here. The power of the place suits me."

"With respect," I started. He gave me a look that put me in mind of both my Father - angry that I would dare challenge him - and my old Naval captain. Thornton had never been able to look at me without sneering, and I would get more clumsy, less competent under his watchful eye.

Both of those men coming to mind was almost enough to stop the words on my tongue, but I pushed forward. "With respect, Solomon, the power of the place might suit you, but if you have spent five years in anger, you cannot possibly be happy. You say you like it, but you also have been consumed by hatred. I don't really see how those two things can be true at the same time."

I blushed. I was confident that I was right, but I was also a little confused about where that particular piece of wisdom had come from. Was it just from the romance novels I loved to read? Or was it because when he laid it out the way he had, it became obvious?

"Hm," Solomon said. He leaned forward, his elbows on his knees. "You are wiser than you look, Gideon."

I swallowed. "Thank you?"

He sighed and sat back up, one hand pushing through and tugging at his hair, calming some of the tangles. His cloak fell back from his shoulder and I saw the litheness of his chest, the swell of the muscles in his arm. He really was beautiful in an unearthly way.

"When I realised how unhappy I was," I started, a little shyly. "I did something about it. Granted, I should have thought it through more, and I could have planned a lot better, but it worked out well enough. Well, I think it did..." I trailed off. I had been planning on leaving the ship before my encounter with both Tate and Ezra. Now my desires may have shifted.

And I'm trapped on an island with a murderous sea witch who wants to use me as bait. So, who knows what the future holds?

Solomon tilted his head again, birdlike and nodded. "Go on."

"I suppose what I realised, when I looked at the portrait of my mother, was that I... I'm allowed to want things, and to have what I want." I cleared my throat, not at all sure this was good advice to be giving to the malicious sea witch opposite me, but I felt that I was getting through to him on some level, and my heart ached to see him smile again.

No one should be unhappy, not even wicked witches.

"So, I took action, even against my Father and all sensible society, and I ran away from home. So that, maybe, somewhere, somehow I could be with a man instead of a woman."

I blushed then, because compared to whatever Solomon had been through, I really sounded like a spoiled brat with very small problems.

"I understand that," Solomon said, his voice quiet.

"I'm really, very pleased to learn a little more about you," I said, smiling at him.

He leaned forward again, shifting his chair closer to the chaise. "You left home, and you ran away. And you found Tate, didn't you?"

"I did..." I leaned forward as well. I licked my lips.

Whatever I had said, he was open now. More vulnerable, we had found something we both understood.

He leaned closer still, and I closed my eyes, my heart pounding.

His lips touched mine, soft and cool, and I kissed him back with raw wanting. My fear translated into a desire to help him, to get through to the man inside. To find the aching heart and see if I could soothe it even a little.

His hand found the back of my skull and caressed the base of it as we deepened the kiss. Emboldened, I put a hand on his bare chest and kneaded gently at it, the way a kitten might.

Solomon made a noise, a low keening which set the hairs on the back of my arms upright. It was a crude noise, raw and unrefined, and seemed to come from the depths of his soul.

I pulled back from the kiss to see his face seeming to crack into despair. His eyes watered, his mouth pulled into a deep grimace.

I reached for his cheek, wanting more than anything in that moment to ease some of his pain, but it seemed to have the opposite effect.

"Don't touch me," he barked. His hand fisted in my hair and yanked my head sharply back from his.

"I'm sorry," I gasped. "I didn't mean -"

"This is ridiculous." He stood, tugging me upright with an abrupt movement. He began to walk, yanking me along with him by the hair. My ankle caught on the chain and I cried out with pain.

"What is it now?" He said, impatiently, then caught sight of the chain. He groaned as if I had done something specifically to anger him. He snapped the fingers of his free hand and the chain came loose from the chaise, wound its way up my body like a snake and pulled my wrists together of its own volition, binding them again.

"Please," I said, desperate and afraid again.

"Shut up," he snapped. "Not another word or I'll put you back to sleep."

"I'm sorry," I said, before my brain registered what he'd just said to me. "I didn't-"

He growled out his frustration and stopped walking. He faced me, put his hand on my forehead and spoke a word I didn't understand.

As I faded into darkness, I sighed.

Maybe I shouldn't have tried to help...

CHAPTER TWENTY-TWO - IN WHICH HELP COMES FROM AN UNEXPECTED DIRECTION

I woke up far too hot, and dry. My face pressed against hot sand.

I was parched, and my heart was racing. The last thing I remembered was Solomon's annoyed face, his hands on my forehead and pulling on my hair.

I sat up and rubbed the back of my head, it was still tender. I hoped he hadn't tugged any out.

Looking around, I found myself on a white sand beach. The waves broke merrily on the sand before me, and on a bank of black rocks to the left. I twisted my body to look behind me. I was on a very small, low island. There were some coconut palms in the centre of it, rocks, beach and nothing else I could make out.

"Oh dear," I breathed to myself.

At least I wasn't still bound. I rubbed my wrists, they'd gone through a lot recently. Looking around some more I took stock.

I wasn't bound physically but I was bound to this island. Solomon had apparently given me no provisions at all. Not even the blanket I'd been half wearing on the chaise. At least it was warmer out here under the sun.

I was alone on a tiny island with just my trousers and some coconut palms.

How did one get a coconut off the tree?

Standing up, I dusted off my trousers and walked towards the small stand of trees. I looked up. I could see them, large and green, but the tree was jolly tall and when I touched the bark, quite smooth.

I took a walk around the outside of the island, it didn't take long. From the beach on the far side from where I woke up I saw a nearby cluster of islands. One of them was much larger than the others and had a tall mountain in the middle of it.

That must be Solomon's island. His house - or, more precisely, his cave - is in there somewhere.

I squinted in the bright afternoon sunlight but I couldn't make out the caves.

How did I get here? And if he wanted to kill me why had he left me here?

Well, the answer to that was easy enough. He didn't want to kill me. He wanted me alive for bait. To bring Tate to him.

And then he'd sink the ship and kill all on board, I assumed.

How foolish of me to think I could reason with him. What had I expected would happen?

Although, even as I berated myself for it, I knew that on some level I *had* reached him. His expressions had shown some true emotion; loss, sadness, pain, but also a glimmer of affection for those days past. And he had kissed me very tenderly. There was something in there that could perhaps be reached by the right person.

Probably not me though. Probably Tate. But Tate is mine, isn't he?

Well, he was Solomon's first.

I sighed and sat down in the shade of the trees.

I needed water and food. Those were the two most pressing problems I had. The island was far too small to have a stream or a spring, so how else could I get fresh water? Rain?

Maybe some rain from the storm the day before would have pooled on the rocks? I hadn't dared walk over the rocks on my survey of the island, but skirted them, sticking to the sand.

It was worth checking. Maybe there'd even be mussels or other shellfish clinging to the rocks.

I gave myself a few more minutes reprieve from the sunshine and got up to investigate. The rocks were sharp and rough under my feet, so I took some time, picking my way over them by the smoothest looking surfaces.

The rocks were uneven, and some of them had tide pools in them. I had loved tide pools as a child. I remembered hours sitting and investigating the denizens of each while my mother kept an eye on me.

None of these tide pools seemed to hold anything edible and further up the rocks all was dry. No lucky rain puddles leftover for me.

Sighing, I looked back towards the ocean and saw a bright flash of colour in the water. Something large and... red?

I picked my way back across the rocks a little faster. It was a very bright red, almost the same colour as my dear lost coat. Was it possible that somehow it had washed up here? On this tiny island? Perhaps Solomon had sent it to me by way of apology. I discarded that thought as soon as I'd had it. There was no evidence at all that Solomon regretted sending me here.

The rocks jutted a couple of feet up from the water, which, at this part of the island, didn't look very shallow. I didn't want to fall in. Today had been hard enough as it was.

Laying flat on the rocks with my head and arms hanging over, I reached into the water to try and reach what clearly was my coat.

Not close enough. I shuffled forward on my belly and leaned down, almost bent in half. There!

I snagged the red fabric with my hand and tried to tug it up. But it seemed to be caught on something.

Grunting, I braced my other hand on the rock and pulled harder. Some of the fabric came out of the water, but it was much heavier than it should have been. Surely it wasn't simply this heavy because it was waterlogged?

A face appeared out of the water, and that's when I saw the problem. My coat was being worn by someone. Or perhaps, something?

The eyes blinked up at me, large and brown, framed by arched eyebrows. The head pushed its way up out of the water and I was face to face with a very pretty man.

For a moment neither of us said anything. We just stared at each other.

He in the water, his arms half in the sleeves of my coat. Me on the rocks, the sun on my back, and my hand holding the hem of the coat up so it dripped down into the gentle surf.

"What are you?" He asked just at the same time I spoke.

"Who are you?"

He smiled then, his face splitting into a warm and very toothy grin. He had a lot of teeth, and they appeared to be pointed.

I swallowed. Solomon's words echoed in my head. *There are creatures here. Merfolk, selkies...*

"I'm Ora of the Green Kelp clan," he said. "What about you?"

"I'm Gideon," I said. "Of the uh, Keene... clan. Why are you wearing my coat underwater?"

"Your what?" He pushed further up and settled on a rock half submerged under the water. He didn't have legs, I saw, he had a long, darkly scaled tail, bedecked with diaphanous fins that floated prettily in the water.

Merfolk. Oh my Lord in Heaven, merfolk are real and I'm speaking to one. What did the old stories say? That if they sang you couldn't resist and they'd lure you into the ocean and drown you?

Saints preserve me.

"You're one of the merfolk," I breathed. I let go of the coat, which slapped wetly against his back, and tried to shuffle back over the rocks.

"You're not," he said. He tipped his head to one side and picked up the coat. "Why did you grab this?"

"It's my coat," I said, automatically. I shifted around and sat up, leaving a good few feet between me and - what had he said his name was? - Ora.

"Coat?" he lifted one of his arms and turned it this way and that, watching the light play over the waterlogged fabric. "Why did you say it was yours?"

"Because it is mine," I cleared my throat. "I bought it."

"What's bought?"

I swallowed. "Um, well, it's clothing, and some people make the clothing, and then people like me, we buy it from them and then we own it."

"A lot of those words mean nothing to me," he said. Then he peered up at me and smiled widely. His eyes sparkled in the sunshine. "But it's all right. I found the, what did you call it?

Coat? In the water after the storm. The colours caught my eye. I wanted it."

"You know what? You can keep it," I said. "My gift to you, don't even worry about it."

"I know what gift is!" Ora smiled and flapped his tail in the water, splashing me with a fine salt spray. I raised a hand to shield my face. "You weren't on this island yesterday, where are you from?"

"I'm, uh, well, it's a bit of a long story," I said. I cleared my throat. "I don't mind telling it to you but..." I trailed off. Asking him outright if he was going to devour or drown me seemed too forthright a question and I didn't want to give him ideas if he hadn't already planned something along those lines. But he seemed friendly enough, and some part of me hoped we could be friends.

"But what?" He frowned a little. "Is it too hot? You could come and sit here, in the water with me?" He shuffled to one side, his magnificent tail glittering in the light. "There's room."

"Oh, well, it is a bit hot," I said. "But I just wanted to know if you were ah, planning on... killing me and eating me?"

I raised my eyebrows and bit my lip.

Ora blinked at me for a moment and then laughed, showing off those rows of terrifyingly pointed teeth. "No! I'm not going to kill you or eat you! What a funny question!" He giggled to himself, and I tried to relax. "I wasn't even going to say anything to you at all, except you grabbed the coat."

"But you knew I was here?"

"Oh yes. I swim past here every day and I notice new things."

"Right, okay. Um, so if you're not going to eat me, can I just ask, what do you eat?"

"Fish, sometimes humans," he said, lightly. "Seaweed, shellfish, all sorts of things really."

My back stiffened and I froze. "Uh, you do eat humans?"

"Yes, but not the ones I've spoken to," he said, casually. "Just like, if they get swept overboard and I happen to be swimming past. If they were going to die anyway."

"Oh, I suppose that is a little better."

He nodded as if consuming humans was a perfectly normal topic of conversation. Maybe for him it was?

"So, you were going to tell me how you got here?"

"The sea witch, Solomon," I said. "He stole me off my ship. Then he stranded me here."

"Why? I mean, Solomon does lots of things I don't understand, so, maybe you could explain it?"

"Well, let's see, he and my Captain had a falling out, and - "

"Did they fall out of the ship?" Ora asked, his brow furrowed.

"Uh, I mean, they had an argument. They used to be friends and now they're enemies. So, Solomon is so angry at my Captain that he made a storm hit the ship, and stole me off of it. With a very large wave."

Ora's eyes had gone very large and wide. "Oh. That sounds like a lot of trouble."

"Indeed," I said. "Before that I was quite happy on the ship, I think. Before *that* I came from an island called Jamaica."

"Jamaica," Ora said, in awe. "Is it bigger than this island?"

I laughed, his innocence was quite charming, really. "Oh yes, much much bigger."

"And what did you say your name was? Garden?"

"Gideon," I said, emphasising the middle e. He repeated it after me and smiled.

"I like you Gideon. Can I stay with you for a while?"

"I... I suppose so," I said. "I'm afraid I haven't any food or water though."

"Fresh water?" Ora asked and I nodded. "I can bring you some, there's a stream on the island over there." He pointed. "Or I could take you there, if you like? If you don't think I'll drown you on the way." He laughed, which made me think he was going to drown me, since he seemed to find it so funny.

But what choice do I have? How exactly can he bring water back, while swimming? And I need water to live.

"I...should like to get to the freshwater," I said.

"Well, then," he held his hand out to me.

I looked into his eyes and my breath caught. Was I really about to do this? Just... jump into the water with an unknowable creature from the sea?

What choice did I have?

"Right, yes," I said. I climbed down off the rocks as carefully as I could. One hand gripped the rocks and when I slipped, Ora caught my other hand. His hand was strong and firm, and I found myself leaning on him more than I'd expected.

Once I lowered myself into the water, he slipped in beside me.

Up close I could see how beautiful he was. He had flowing brown curls, his skin was clear with a tinge of green around the edges. His eyes were large and warm brown, and he had the longest, thickest eyelashes I'd ever seen.

If his teeth weren't quite so terrifying I'd want to kiss him.

"Hold onto me," he said. Moving closer to me and then turning away.

"Um." I put my hands on his shoulders, feeling the taut muscles under his skin, which was surprisingly warm for all he appeared to be a fish-being.

"More than that," he said, half turning to look at me over his shoulder. "I don't want to lose you, Gideon. This coat does make me swim a little slower than normal, but I can still swim quite fast."

"Right," I said. Tentatively, I lifted my arm over his shoulder and folded it in front of his chest. The other hand I slipped under the water, under his other arm to grasp my own hand and lace my fingers together. "Is this all right?"

"I think so," he said. "We'll find out together. I've never done this with a human before."

"I've never done this with a merman either," I said. I was nervous, but something about Ora felt safe to me.

Much more than being with Solomon. Something in me just seemed to know he wouldn't hurt me, despite the stories I'd heard.

"Mer-man?" He asked. "I'm not a man."

"You're not? But you... your chest..." I stammered.

"Merfolk," he said.

Saints preserve me, I'm trusting my life to a merman who doesn't know what a man is.

CHAPTER TWENTY-THREE - IN WHICH THE GREY KELPIE APPROACHES THE ISLAND

ate had stayed up much of the night at the helm with Ezra, until the storm died off shortly before dawn and they'd both taken to their beds, leaving the ship at anchor. Collapsing into bed, Tate was relieved that he was so exhausted from the night's activities that he fell asleep almost immediately.

His sleep was largely oblivion until he dreamed of Solomon.

At first, the dream was a pleasant one, the two of them side by side on the deck of the Grey Kelpie on a clear and sunshine soaked day. Solomon wore a crisp white shirt and knee length grey breeches.

Solomon took his hand and it was warm and Tates's chest filled with happiness.

Then with a start he recalled the events of the past. He had cheated Solomon on a lucrative deal, kept the spoils for himself and when Solomon had found out they'd fought. Things had become violent.

Beside him Solomon seemed to change, he got taller, and his skin turned from his usual mid brown to a strange unworldly grey.

"I have the boy," he'd said, in a voice older and with more gravitas than Tate remembered.

"The boy?" Tate asked, but then, with another jolt, he thought of Gideon.

"Yes, that boy," Solomon said. "You shall have to come close to get him back, if you think you can that is. Of course, if your *feelings* for him," he put an ironic emphasis on the word feelings, "are anything like what you felt for me, then you can just sail away."

"No, I can't," Tate said.

"You can, and you likely will," Solomon said. "Your heart is unchanged, all you really wish for is more money, more gold to stow away for your retirement."

"I'm not, it's not like that."

"I can smell you on the wind, and I shall have my way. Come and find him, I dare you."

Then Solomon laughed, and it was a sound that had more in common with the crying of gulls than an ordinary human voice.

Tate woke with a start, his heart pounding, his hand fisted in the bedclothes. "Fuck."

"It's a trap," Ezra said.

"I'm well aware that it's a trap," Tate growled. "But what do you suggest we do? Leave him there? With the sea witch? If Solomon sees us sailing away, then do you think he'd have any reason to keep Gideon alive?"

Ezra huffed his breath out of his nose and tapped his fingers on the table.

They stood in the captain's cabin, a half hour after Tate had woken. They both stared at a map of the Splintered Islands spread between them. The group of islands had one large central piece of land, and then a dozen or more smaller islands scattered around. These islands were of various sizes.

Ezra stared at the map hopelessly. They knew the Southern side of the island group housed a colony of merfolk. The Eastern side had an extensive coral reef, the Northern side had many rocks hidden just below the water's surface.

"The Western side is the only possible approach," he said.

"Yes, which means that Solomon will know that's the approach we will take, and he will do whatever it takes to destroy this ship." Tate ran both hands through his hair and groaned. "What should we do? All I can think of is getting Gideon back. Every time I try to come up with a plan I imagine the terrible things Solomon might be doing to him."

"We're still not even sure if he has Gideon, or if Gideon simply... drowned in the storm." Ezra said, tapping his finger on the table.

"I'm sure he does," Tate said. "My dream-"

"Could simply be a lure," Ezra said.

"The weather has been fine and calm," Tate said. "A friendly breeze and easy sailing. We know Solomon can control the weather, if he wanted to swamp the boat he could have sent another storm. Instead he invites us, as plain as if he'd sent a paper invitation."

The silence stretched between them.

"Are you willing to gamble on that?" Ezra asked finally.

Tate averted his eyes and ground his teeth. He sighed. "We both have feelings for the boy, I know that. I'm not sure I could live with myself if we abandoned him. If there's a chance we can get him back, then I want to do it."

"So that we can share him?" Ezra asked. He waited until Tate looked up and locked eyes, the air seemed to crackle between them.

The ship's cat sauntered into the room, looked up at the both of them and meowed loudly. There was no denying the cat was annoyed at something. Ezra shifted his weight from one side to the other.

"I don't know how it would work," Tate said. He raised a hand palm up towards Ezra - a gesture of peace, an offering of understanding. "One thing at a time, and the first thing must be getting him back."

Ezra hesitated and then put his hand in Tate's and shook it. "All right. We could always send out a long boat? It's a little less obvious, less of a risk than the ship itself."

Tate nodded and exhaled loudly. "Not a bad idea."

Zeb jumped up onto the map and they both turned to watch as he walked in a circle and sat down on the image of the main island. One paw was outstretched towards the Southern side of the island group.

"If we take a small boat, we can approach from one of the other directions," Tate said, thoughtfully. "Merfolk aren't likely to bother a longboat are they?"

"I really have no idea," Ezra said, dryly. "I'm sensible and have always avoided places where merfolk are rumoured to be."

"As ever, I am grateful for your helpful assistance, First Mate."

Ezra gave Tate a wide, toothy grin. "Come on, Cap'n, let's plan this properly. Who are we taking with us, who is staying aboard, and what is the plan of attack?"

It took two hours, but soon they had moved the Grey Kelpie and were lowering a longboat into the water, well stocked with swords and guns. Joseph had been left in charge of the ship while Tate was on his mission, and they were taking Shem and three others others in the boat with them as a raiding party.

They all rowed as quietly as they could. Not a one of them willing to break the silence as they approached the Splintered Isles.

CHAPTER TWENTY-FOUR - IN WHICH GIDEON AND ORA EXPLORE

The water was a pleasant temperature, and holding onto Ora so close wasn't unpleasant exactly. My heart pounded in my chest, sure I was about to die, but at the same time, I wanted to trust this strange mercreature.

Ora nodded, flicked his tail and dove into the water away from the rocks.

Clinging to him, I took a quick breath and held it as he dived underwater. The drag of the water threatened to pull me off his back, so I held on as tightly as I could.

He flipped his tail powerfully beneath me and we shot through the water fast. I closed my eyes and buried my face against his neck, into the collar of my coat, concentrating on holding on.

We broke the surface and I took a ragged breath. Opening my eyes I saw we were far from the tiny island already, heading towards one of the nearby larger ones, but not the one with the mountain on it.

"Hold your breath," Ora said. I took a deep breath and he

dove again. His tail beat the water and I screwed my eyes shut and clung to him.

We broke the surface once more, there was a beach very close by and the water around us was blue and light, rather than the dark, deep blue we'd swum through.

Quick as a fish, he turned in my arms, his nose practically touching mine. "Here we are," he said.

Close enough to kiss...

There was a bump as he slid onto the sand below the surf and my weight landed me on top of him. My chest pressed against his, my legs straddling his tail. He was very firm below me, his body hard muscle and slippery scaling. My cock pulsed once in my once again salt water soaked trousers.

My mouth was dry and my eyes blurred with salt, my breathing was fast, as if it had been me that'd swum so far and so fast.

"I should..." I let go of him and slid off sideways. "Thank you, that was very kind of you."

"Are you all right?" Ora asked. He squeezed my shoulder with one hand.

"Yes, yes, I'm all right." I stood up, unsteady on the soft sand. My knees shook a little from travelling partially underwater, and from being on top of such a gorgeous, lithe, muscled man.

No, it was merfolk. Not man. I must remember that.

"Careful," he called out, laughing again. He stood up, and I blinked, swiped my hand over my eyes - which didn't help because my arm was soaked with salt water too - he was standing up on two legs.

Aside from my wet coat, he was utterly naked as he stood in the shallow surf. He was well endowed and just as beautiful with legs as with a tail. Even more beautiful truly, as it was less alien.

My knees shook and I would have fallen if he hadn't caught me by the elbow.

"I said be careful," he said, with a mock stern tone. I had to laugh, Ora was so cheerful, it was incredibly refreshing.

I felt at ease, relaxed in his company. Like I didn't have to try to impress him, or be polite, or try and convince him not to kill me.

"Sorry," I said. "I suppose, holding onto you while you swim was exhilarating, but it was a little bit terrifying as well."

"You're safe with me," he said. I looked into his eyes and saw the earnestness there. I nodded.

"I know. It's just... you're naked under the coat. Um, would you mind closing it up?"

"Why?" Ora asked. He looked down at himself and then at me. "Oh, do you cover your genitals?"

"Uh, yes, humans all do... cover their... genitals," I stammered. My cheeks warmed.

"You've gone pinker than before," he said. He let go of my elbow and pulled the coat around himself. "Why?"

"I'm... I guess I'm embarrassed."

"Because of my genitals?" I carefully focused my gaze on his eyes and nodded. We were almost exactly the same height.

"Y-yes, Ora. Because of your genitals."

"Sorry about it," he said.

"Oh, I don't want you to feel sorry about it, it's fine, it's just me," I said, quickly. "The fact is, that, um, you're very attractive to me."

"That's kind of you."

"Um, if you're not a man," I started, wondering how to ask

what I needed to without further complicating things. "Is it all right for me to call you a him? He and him are how I've been thinking of you, but if there's another option, I'd be happy to use it instead."

"You worry about strange things," he said. "But he is all right. Under the sea they call me they. They and them."

"They and them," I nodded and smiled at them. "I'll remember. I want to use what makes you most comfortable. I'm a he and him," I added, quickly.

Ora nodded once.

"It's this way," they said, lightly, turned on their heel and led the way up the beach and into the underbrush. This island had coconut palms as well, but also large shrubs and strange flowering bushes. It all looked much more like there was water flowing somewhere - not that I had doubted Ora, exactly - but it was a nice reassurance.

Ora hummed as they walked, a very pleasant melody. They had a fine range and I swallowed, for I very much wanted to hear more of that singing voice, but the old stories echoed in my ears. *Merfolk are sirens, their song is their lure...*

"Here," they said. They stopped and smiled back at me, utterly open and guileless, and I smiled back without hesitation.

They had brought me to a spring with a small waterfall. Bright tropical flowers bloomed on either side of the small rock bank the water fell from, and there were even some ferns low to the ground.

"This is beautiful," I breathed, my hand coming up to my mouth.

"I just knew you'd like it," Ora said. They reached for my hand and squeezed it, then brought my hand up to their mouth to kiss the back of it. "Come on then, don't you want a drink?"

If they're not going to make a big thing over kissing my hand, then it doesn't have to be a big thing, I told myself. *Just go with it, they don't understand about human manners and etiquette... Which means I don't have to, either, doesn't it?*

The thought was incredibly freeing. I felt my shoulders relax and I let out a heavy breath, feeling lighter and bubbling with surprised levity.

"Wonderful," I said, allowing them to tug me towards the spring.

"It's best from up here," they said. They crouched on the bank beside the waterfall and cupped their hand under it, then offered me their hand to drink from.

I didn't hesitate, just leaned in and drank the fresh spring water from their palm.

"Oh, that is divine," I said. I squeezed their hand. "Hold me? I want to put my mouth under there."

"All right," they said. They held me across their lap as I drank from the waterfall, and soon I had my fill.

Once my thirst was satiated it occurred to me that I was lying across their lap. And they had no trousers on at all.

Well, what's the problem with that? I'm not in polite society, here. They won't think less of me if I enjoy it. They're very comfortable with their body, and don't seem to be anything but flattered that I find them attractive, after all. Maybe merfolk don't have shame. That's a fascinating thought.

I sat up, still very close to them and looked into their eyes. They smiled back and I realised that in human form, they had ordinary human teeth. It was a relief, because it meant I wouldn't be afraid to kiss them, which I very much wanted to do.

But we didn't have to do that right away, of course. I reached up to touch their cheek, which was cool, but not as cool as they'd been in merform.

"What is it?" They asked, leaning their cheek into my hand a little.

"You're... just, astoundingly handsome," I said, softly.

"Thank you," they said. "I think you're the most beautiful thing I've ever seen, well, after your coat, that is."

I had to laugh at that, and they joined in, their hand moving to my waist and lightly stroking me there.

"This coat is ruined," I said. I let my hand slip down to the collar, which was warped and pulled from the water. The red colour was already starting to bleed out of the fabric, and as it dried I was sure the lining would shrink.

"Ruined? I don't think so," they said, and glanced down at it. "It's changing so much. I find it fascinating."

Fascinating? I'd use that word to describe Ora themself. Their presence is intoxicating, I could definitely get used to this.

"Have you ever," they started, and then stopped. They ran their tongue over their teeth. I'd not seen them hesitate before. It piqued my interest.

"Have I ever what?"

"I have no idea how humans mate," they said, slowly. "Is it, is it something you ever do for fun?"

"Oh, yes," I said. I caught their hand and brought it to my cheek, encouraging them to stroke it. "Yes, we do. And recently, I've learned quite a lot about how two men, or, uh, three, can have fun together."

Ora's face lit up and they sat straighter, moving closer to me. "Really? And men means... like you? Like this body?" they gestured down at their bare legs and what lay between them.

I nodded, my mouth dry again but this time not because I was thirsty for water.

"Yes," I said, softly.

"So, that's the kind of thing you like?" Their hand went to my neck, and they stroked the faint bruise there - Tate's and Ezra's marks, one over the other. I shivered some involuntarily.

"Yes," I said again. "What kind of thing do you like?"

"Well." They trailed their fingers down my chest, tracing soft swirling patterns on my skin. It felt warm and exciting. "Under the waves we sometimes get a little wild, and I like to mate with all sorts of different folk, but you..." They breathed out softly, I felt the warmth of their breath on my shoulder as they leaned in, placing kisses here and there on my skin. "You are the most beautiful and interesting thing I've ever seen."

"I might say the same about you," I smiled. I tipped my head up and caught their lips with mine. Kissing them sent sparks and tingles through me, and with a soft moan I wrapped my hands around their waist and pulled them closer against me.

They smiled. "Can I touch your hair? It's almost as bright as the coat."

"Yes," I nodded and shifted, climbing into their lap and stroking my hands over their chest. I couldn't help but compare them to Tate and Ezra. They weren't as tall or broad as either of them, their muscles were lithe and firm, but their waist was narrow and straddling them felt as natural as - I had trouble thinking of when I'd felt more natural, or at home - sitting in the garden and reading for hours? No. It didn't matter.

I felt comfortable with Ora, with touching them and with them touching me, as if some part of my soul recognised them and was at home in their company.

Their hands moved to my hair, still damp from the swim

earlier, and they combed their fingers through it with a gentle movement. The tug - so different to Solomon's roughness - felt incredible and I rocked my hips, grinding myself against their cock, which I could feel pressing against me.

"That feels really good," I murmured. Ora kissed up my throat and softly bit me, so gentle it didn't hurt, just made the kisses that much more interesting.

"You taste marvellous," they replied. "Every time I touch you I feel such pleasure. I want more."

"I need," I murmured, then cleared my throat. "If you... if you want to do this with me, I'll need to take my trousers off."

"Yes, that would be good," Ora said. They gripped me by the waist, steadying me as I went up on my knees to pull my trousers open. As I stripped them off and kicked them away, Ora kept hold of me so I didn't overbalance. I settled myself back in their lap.

I should have felt wanton, practically riding the merfolk out in a glade with a waterfall... but there was no one around to see, and I felt nothing but affection and joy.

I kissed them again, smiling into it as the sparks shot through me again. Ora's hand found my cock and then they were stroking me with slow, delicious tugs that had me moaning into their mouth. Their other hand buried in my hair, gently massaging my scalp and tugging my hair softly.

I wrapped a hand around their cock and stroked it, and moved my other hand behind to stretch myself open, groaning loudly.

No one to hear but the birds and butterflies.

"Let me," they murmured, and took over. I was startled to feel a slickness to their fingers as they slipped inside me.

"Magic?" I asked, breathless already.

They nodded once, pulling back to meet my eyes. "My kind have certain secretions when we want them..." They licked their lips and kissed me again, at the same instant they scissored their fingers and I cried out into their mouth. "Is it too much?" They asked, eyes wide with concern. Their fingers stilled inside me and I stifled a whine.

"No, no it's wonderful," I said, shaking my head. "Please continue."

"You talk so strange," they said, chuckling. Their fingers took up their movement again, curling and pressing inside me to make me cry out again.

I wrapped my arms around their shoulders and pressed my forehead to theirs.

Soon I was throbbing and squirming with need.

"Please Ora, I need you, your cock inside me," I gasped. I reached down to stroke their cock and lifted my hips to guide them in as they withdrew their fingers.

They kissed me as they surged up inside me. I sank down until they were completely buried inside me, and I moaned louder still, hearing my sounds echo back off the tree trunks and the rocks of the waterfall.

Ora wrapped their arms tight around me and lay back, pulling me on top of their chest. I laughed a little, feeling them inside me, how easy it had all been, how free of shame and humiliation - it went to my head the way champagne bubbles might.

I hitched one of my knees up to align with their hip and rolled myself onto them, making them moan in a curiously high pitched way.

"Ohhh, that's it," they groaned. "You're so warm - hot really, it's so good."

"You feel exquisite to me," I replied, and then giggled, because what a pretentious word to use in that moment? But it was accurate.

Good wasn't a word that would describe what I was feeling, or how perfect it all seemed to be going. I had to use more complex vocabulary to express it, or I would be doing Ora a disservice.

Ora giggled too, and then our mouths crashed together and we kissed and moved until they were bucking their hips, arching their back and filling me.

I sat up a little and they stroked me, although I hardly needed it. As soon as their fingers closed on my cock I was climaxing hard, squeezing tight with the muscles inside me so they moaned all over again.

Collapsing back onto their chest, I lay there and panted heavily.

"Magical," I said. "You're utterly magical."

"You are my favourite thing," they said. They turned their head and kissed my hair, causing my toes to curl from affection and happiness.

I reached up to stroke their hair, which had dried into brown spiral curls. They hummed happily and closed their eyes.

I shifted off him and we curled up together in a bed of moss. I fell asleep almost instantly.

CHAPTER TWENTY-FIVE - IN WHICH IT IS MOST DEFINITELY A TRAP

*R*owing the longboat to shore made Tate nervous for many, many reasons, but the chief one was that he couldn't watch the island. He was staring out to sea and sweating in the hot sun and worrying.

The men were all quiet as they rowed, just the sound of the oars dipping in and out of the water, the gentle splash of waves against the side, and the cry of seabirds every now and then.

They had chosen to approach via the Southern side of the island, sending Joseph to sail the Grey Kelpie towards the Western approach and anchor far enough out that Solomon would think they were biding their time.

There were numerous small islands on this side, some of them barely large enough to hold a coconut palm, and some larger. They made navigation a little more difficult but Tate hoped they were providing cover as well.

"I can't see anything in the water," Ezra said, low, breaking the silence.

"That's good."

All the men knew there were supposed to be merfolk on this

side of the island, and one of the reasons they'd stayed quiet was to avoid attention from below.

It felt like walking through a dark alley when you knew enemies were after you, Tate mused. Attack could come from any direction.

But his heart stayed resolute. They had to confront Solomon and rescue Gideon.

Or even better, they could rescue Gideon and avoid Solomon altogether and steal off as fast as possible.

That was definitely his preference, if only they could make it work.

After what felt like an age, Ezra spoke up again. "Mainland."

Tate shored his oar and turned to watch as they moved into shallower waters. Shem stepped out of the boat to wade through the gentle surf and guide the boat to the dry sand.

"So far, so good," Tate murmured as they stepped out of the water.

Looking up from the beach they were close to the foot of the mountain, which was thick with trees and plants. There was no clear path for how to reach Solomon's lair.

"Where now, Cap?" Shem asked.

The crew busied themselves, sheathing swords and picking up machetes for hacking through the forest.

He caught Ezra's eye.

Ezra looked pissed off, and uncomfortably warm in his signature black shirt and trousers. Tate nodded at him, and they led the way up the beach, the others a step or two behind them.

Tate nodded up the beach. "We head for the mountain, see how far we can get before he notices us."

"It's a brilliant plan, really," a voice came from behind them. "Only one thing wrong with it, actually."

Solomon stood in the water, next to the longboat. He cut a dramatic figure, his long black cloak swirling in the surf, his chest bare, his cheekbones seeming to sparkle in the bright sunlight.

He grinned in the way a shark would if you were bleeding in the open water.

"Fuck," Tate said. He drew his sword in the same breath.

"I already know you're here." Solomon continued, as if someone had asked him to elaborate. His eyes locked on Tate's.

"Where is he?" Ezra shouted, surprising both Tate and Solomon.

Solomon's eyebrows shot up and he gave a cold laugh. "Oh, I see that perhaps the Governor's son is valuable to more than just the Captain? How fascinating."

"Governor's son?" Tate whispered.

Finally, he had the explanation for why Gideon had been using a false name. He was the son of the Governor of Kingston - of course he was. No wonder he had such expensive taste in clothing.

"The boy is here, on the Splintered Islands, you could probably find him before he starves or dies of thirst, assuming you can get off this beach." Solomon spread his arms wide to either side of him and laughed again, this laugh seemed to carry on the wind and echo back to the pirates.

Tate shivered despite the hot sun beating down on them.

"You've changed, Solomon," he said, summoning all his bravery to sound confident and unruffled.

"Aye, I'm far stronger than when we last stood face to face." Solomon moved forward, out of the water. A scattering of blue shelled crabs followed in his wake.

"Strong, maybe, but less human," Tate said. "What've you done with the boy?"

"Why do you care so much?" Solomon hissed. "Do you love him?"

Above them, clouds rapidly covered the sun, and the beach grew darker and colder. Tate swallowed hard, but made his way back down the beach, going to meet Solomon.

"Captain," Ezra murmured. "Perhaps this is not the best -"

"If you love him, you'd better tell him that it means nothing," Solomon spat. "You told me you loved me once, and look where that got me. Stranded here! And you sailing off in our ship and doing whatever you please."

He gestured at the mountain behind Tate, and a bolt of lightning forked down from the sky, causing all the pirates to startle.

The sky broke and rain came pouring down on them, hard and heavy.

"Fight me, Solomon!" Tate shouted over the sound of the rain. "This is between you and me, not Gideon. Not any of these men. If you have a grudge with me? I'm right here. But let them all go, Gideon too."

Solomon laughed again, stalking ever closer to Tate.

Ezra and the other pirates closed in, a semi circle to either side of their captain. Solomon glanced at them. "Hardly a fair fight, is it?"

"Stand down-" Tate started to say. Solomon pointed at the sky and then at the sand at his feet. Lightning struck inches from Tate's boots and he fell backwards, swearing. The others were similarly scattered.

With a sweeping gesture of his other hand, Solomon called a

wave to crash up the beach, swamping the fallen men and swirling harmlessly around his thighs.

Tate struggled to his feet, turned and grabbed Ezra's arm to haul him upright. Ezra coughed out water as the wave receded back into the ocean. Tate let go and turned back, levelling his sword at the witch.

"Enough games, Solomon," Tate growled. "You and me, right here."

"I said it wasn't a fair fight," Solomon said. "I meant for you."

With that he brought both hands over his head and seemed to pull down even more rain. Monsoon heavy, it destroyed what visibility Tate had. There was a huge boom of thunder above them, and lightning struck Tate's sword. Instantly the metal superheated and burned his hand, he swore, dropped it and reached for his dagger.

Ezra stepped forward, lunging as if to plant his rapier into Solomon's chest, but he was too slow. Solomon let out a yell and a sudden wind beat Ezra back from him, sending him tumbling over the sand like a leaf.

Tate thought he saw a flash of red, bright, brilliant red. Heart racing, he tore his eyes away to focus on Solomon again.

"I have waited for this moment for too long," the witch hissed. Tate knew then just how powerful his magic had grown, because he shouldn't have been able to hear Solomon over the pouring rain and the continuing rumble of thunder. But his voice was as clear as if he were whispering in Tate's ear. "I want to make you suffer, the way you made me suffer, all these years alone, all these years..."

Tate struck out with his dagger, slashing the air and hoping to meet his mark.

"That boy? He's nothing, barely knows who he is, and to think, you'd come back for him and not me? It's preposterous."

"He's different," Tate said, through gritted teeth. He could see the shape of Solomon through the rain. He surged forward and stabbed at it, and fell on his face, as the shape was nothing but an illusion. "He doesn't use his love as a weapon, he doesn't grasp and cling and play mind games with me. Not like you did."

"You're not different, though," Solomon taunted. "You're the same selfish prick you ever were."

He pushed up from the wet sand and whirled, peering and trying to see the witch.

"Now I have you," Solomon hissed, and Tate could hear the triumph in his voice. Then something closed around him, a thin, cold snake vining around his shoulders, pinning his arms to the side.

He squirmed, feeling the magicked chain cutting into his muscles as it pulled his arms close into his sides. He dropped his dagger, swearing as he felt more of the chain crawl snake like up his legs, pinioning those too.

"No sense in fighting it, Tate," Solomon's voice whispered, almost tenderly, but the nastiness was still present in his tone. "You're mine now."

Tate had no idea where Ezra or the others had gone.

And that flash of red? Maybe he'd imagined it. He struggled, but it was hopeless.

He was just a man, he couldn't fight magic.

"*T*here's no sense in -"

Solomon's voice cut off abruptly.

"That's it," I urged Ora. Ora stood beside me in the water, wearing my red coat and singing. It was a soft, lilting tune being sung by surely the most talented singer in the world.

I couldn't make out the words, but the music had an instant effect on the beach. For a start, the mad, localised monsoon eased into a gentle drizzle, making the bodies on the beach visible again.

"Target Solomon, though," I whispered to Ora and I heard them sing Solomon's name.

Solomon, who had stopped moving the moment Ora's voice rang out, seemed to fall asleep. His head nodded forward, and then he slumped onto his knees, waist deep in a high tide that was quickly subsiding back into the ocean.

The chain that had been magically binding Tate loosened and fell away, and I fought the desire to rush to his side. Ora had warned me, though, that it wouldn't be safe until they gave the signal.

The clouds above drifted away and the sun came out again. I could see Ezra, lying on the beach, covered in sand as if he had rolled in it. Scattered wide were more crew, in various states of half drowned and dashed against the shore.

Ora took a step towards Solomon, still singing the strange but undeniably beautiful song. My heart filled with light and happiness listening to it, even though Ora had me stopper my ears with seaweed.

Ora waved me forward and I rushed to Tate's side. He swayed as if drunk, a beatific smile on his face. I reached up to caress his cheek with one hand and his eyes swivelled to mine.

"Come on," I said, tugging him down the beach.

Ora and I had found the longboat some ways out - Solomon must've sent it away so the pirates couldn't escape. Hauling it back in had been difficult but Ora was surprisingly strong. Maybe not so surprising, given they could change forms at will.

Once I had Tate moving towards the boat, I rushed to Ezra, sparing a quick look at Ora, who stood behind Solomon, one hand on the top of his head.

"Ezra, wake up!" I cried, shaking his shoulder. He blinked at me, as if he had merely been napping on the beach. He sat up and kissed me hard, one hand moving around my shoulders. I melted into it for a moment before shaking him off. "No time, you idiot. Got to get out of here!"

Ezra nodded and stood, between us we roused the other members of the crew and loaded them into the longboat as fast as possible.

Tate sat in the front, smiling dreamily.

Once they were all in, I called out to Ora, who crouched over Solomon who was now lying in the sand. At my shout, Ora stopped singing, rushed towards the boat and nodded at me.

"You get in too, I can push the boat," they said. I clambered in, and sat, watching the prone form of Solomon anxiously as Ora shoved the boat into the water. Then they transformed and swam behind us as we rapidly went deeper.

I pulled the seaweed out from my ears and tossed it into the water.

Ezra had his eyes fixed on the beach as well, so I shifted over to Tate. "Tate, are you all right?" I asked.

Ora had mentioned that their song might work better on some people than others. And Solomon would definitely have been focusing a lot of power on him. Perhaps the combination of magic had an effect on him?

It was so good to see him again, I pressed my hand against his chest. "Tate," I said again. "Captain, please."

The boat hit a wave and Tate seemed to shake his head, as if coming out of a dream, and his eyes found mine. His goofy, drunken smile faded and he smiled just for me. "Gideon," he said, his voice wavering and unsure. "There you are. I thought I'd lost you. I lost..."

He closed his mouth, wrapped me in his arms and pulled me against him in a tight hug, which I returned happily - all my previous sense of humiliation or embarrassment at being physical with another man seemed just a memory now, and I felt confident in hugging him back.

I kissed his cheek and we held each other until I heard Ezra cough nearby. I pulled back some, leaving one arm around Tate and reached for Ezra with the other hand. He took hold of me and tugged me towards him.

It was undoubtedly awkward in the small space, the other members of the crew variously watching or pretending not to notice. When I glanced at him Shem gave me a wink and a nod... his approval.

I leaned over and kissed Ezra. Although most of our kisses had been about possession or urgency, this one was all reassurance. His hand squeezed mine almost painfully and I squeezed it back. A soft noise came from the back of his throat.

Then I settled back, leaning against Tate and holding Ezra's hand as the longboat sped towards the ship.

The ship came into view on the Western side of the islands, and the sight of it made me catch my breath. I had come to think of the Grey Kelpie as home, and there was no mistaking that my heart had missed it.

How strange, that so recently, I thought I wanted to leave it altogether.

I moved away from my two pirate lovers and to the back of the boat. I had already moved around so much on this brief trip that the other crew simply shifted aside as I did this, and Shem even offered his hand to steady me. I crouched at the back of the longboat and looked over the back.

Ora's hands gripped the back of the boat, so I reached down and tapped one of their wrists.

They stopped beating their tail so furiously and their head bobbed up out of the water. They smiled wide to see me, and I couldn't help but smile back. Behind me, I heard the men shift uncertainly, and one made a soft prayer.

"The ship's just over there," I said, and pointed towards it. They looked past me and nodded.

"I see it."

"Thank you for this." Even though their mouth was full of pointed teeth, I leaned over and kissed them gently. They kissed me back with a closed mouth.

"Of course, Gid," they said. They pushed themself up out of the water until their elbows rested on the back of the boat and beat their tail almost lazily, coasting us towards the Grey Kelpie more gently.

"What is ... who is this, Gideon?" Tate asked.

"This is Ora," I said, smiling and tousling Ora's damp curls. "They're one of the merfolk."

"Heaven and the saints preserve us," Ezra said faintly. I looked over at him, and saw his eyes were wide. "The siren's song stopped Solomon, didn't it?"

Tate swore under his breath.

"It did."

We reached the Grey Kelpie, and Ora pushed the boat to where the rope ladder hung down.

"Are you coming?" I asked Ora as the others hurried up the ladder and onto the ship deck.

"I've never been on a ship before," Ora said, their voice full of wonder and curiosity.

"Assuming it's all right with the Captain," I added quickly. I looked at Tate, who had been watching me, bemused. He shrugged.

"We owe Ora our lives, I believe," he said. "They are welcome on the Grey Kelpie if they wish to come."

Delighted, I nodded. "Yes, please come on board, Ora."

They swam under the boat and resurfaced at the foot of the rope ladder, hanging on with one hand as they shifted forms. Tate helped me up to the ladder and I went before Ora, instructing them on how to use it.

Ezra helped me onto the deck - having been one of the first up the ladder. Once I was on board he caught me in his arms and kissed me properly, a soft noise from the back of his throat betraying his worry for me, and his relief that we were reunited.

I pulled back to check on Ora's progress. Behind them I could hear Tate urging them on.

"That's it, one more, then climb over the side."

I went to catch Ora as they scrambled over the side, my poor, waterlogged coat dripping off their shoulders. They landed half in my arms, their hands on my shoulders and we shared a laugh.

"What's that?" they asked, pointing behind me at one of the masts.

"That's the mast, the large bit of fabric is the mainsail, it's how the ship moves with the wind," I said.

"There's something wrong," Shem said, breathlessly, appearing beside Ezra.

Tate climbed onto deck behind me and Ora. "What is it, Shem?"

"I can't find... there's no one at helm, no one on deck," he said. "Anton's gone below to look there, but I don't like it, Captain."

"Fan out, everyone," Tate ordered. "Be alert, keep your weapons drawn. It could be Solomon."

There was a shout from below. Tate and Ezra took off at a run to the stairway that led below. I followed, Ora close behind me.

Solomon couldn't possibly be here on the ship, could he?

CHAPTER TWENTY-SEVEN - IN WHICH
A TRAITOR IS REVEALED

Tate led the way down the stairs. Ezra hissed at him, tried to take hold of his shoulder. "You're too valuable, stay back, Tate." Tate ignored this and barrelled on regardless.

Shem had pushed his way in front of me when we got to the narrow passage, and I let him, for I was utterly unarmed. Noticing this, he shoved a dagger into my hand, and then descended. I followed, clutching the dagger but uncertain if I could actually use it if it came to that.

The brig was full of people. I noticed Sagorika, apparently asleep on the bench, the rest of the crew arranged around, sleeping or unconscious.

Tate seemed to be searching for the key, Ezra rattled the door of the brig uselessly.

"I had hoped it wouldn't come to this," Joseph's voice cut through the confusion, and silence fell as we turned to look at him. He had appeared from deeper inside the ship, near to me. I took an instinctive step back and pressed against Ora, who slipped a hand around my waist.

"Joseph, what's the meaning of this?" Tate seemed to grow taller, his face becoming thunderous with anger.

"My master bids you greetings," he said.

"Your master?" Ezra's sword glinted in the dim light.

"Aye, my master, Solomon," he said. He drew something from his shirt, which glowed with an unholy light - green and sickly, some amulet or talisman that I wasn't sure if I'd noticed him wearing before or not.

"Joseph, put that down," Tate said. His voice was full of command and authority - I certainly would have obeyed him - but Joseph smiled unpleasantly. Just the same kind of smile Solomon himself was fond of.

"Why should I put it down when it's a gift?" he asked. His voice cracked slightly, he sounded strained.

"That thing is powerful," Ora whispered in my ear. "It's hurting him, sucking the life out of his body like a leech."

"You don't have to do this," I said, impulsively. "Please, Joseph, you can be free of him."

Joseph's gaze pulled from Tate and locked itself on my face. His smile pulled wider, it looked painful now. His eyes glowed with reflected light as he pulled the bauble free from his neck and held it up.

Oh, I wish I hadn't spoken.

"You," he hissed. "Gideon. You're the one."

"Don't you speak to him," Tate thundered. He took a step closer to Joseph and froze as Joseph thrust the amulet forward and sparks flew off it.

"Stay back! You don't get to order me around any more, *Captain.* Captain Useless, Captain Good-for-nothing! Solomon has shown me real power."

"How?" Ezra demanded. "You've not left the ship, he's not left the island."

"He doesn't have to," Joseph sneered. "In my dreams he visits me, teaching me all sorts of things, and then this morning, I woke up with this."

He shook the amulet and more sparks flew to land sizzling on the wooden deck.

Ora's arm around me pulled me close against their body, backing away from Joseph.

"Joseph, please," I said. "I know it doesn't have to come to this, if we could just talk this through."

"Don't be ridiculous," Joseph laughed meanly. "Talking? What will talking do?"

"If you were content, you'd see that whatever Solomon has offered you isn't worth it," I said. My mind was racing and I really had no idea if what I was saying was true or not, but I had to try. Joseph seemed to be angry, and hurting. Maybe we could get through to him.

I felt something against my leg and startled, looking down, but it was just Zeb, winding around my ankle to welcome me back onto the ship. He looked back up at me with a very pleased expression.

Now's not the time to be distracted.

Ezra darted forward.

"No!" I cried, as Joseph thrust the amulet at him. Ezra stopped just in time, the amulet fell short, swinging scant inches from his chest. Ezra, growling with frustration, took a step back.

"What does that thing even do?" Tate asked. "Did Solomon tell you to do this?"

"Aye, first it allowed me to direct the crew down here, and

sent them to sleep," Joseph said. "But now it has only one purpose left."

His eyes cut to me and I cringed back against Ora's chest. "I could sing," Ora whispered. I shook my head. There were too many people in too small a place. Besides, I was afraid of what Ora's song might do to an amulet so powerful it could put a dozen people under its control.

"And what is that purpose? To kill me I suppose?" Tate asked, his voice unwavering.

Instead of answering, Joseph laughed, a dry cackle which sent shivers across my skin. He pulled his arm back and threw the amulet at me.

In the same instant:

Zeb yowled and leapt into the air from my feet

Tate cried "NO!" loud enough to rattle the rafters

Ezra stepped neatly forward and ran Joseph through with his sword

Ora wrapped their arms around me and spun us, pushing me against the wall

For an instant, it seemed time slowed to a snail's pace, and I took in all these actions, before I was facing the wrong way, Ora's body shielding me from whatever had just happened.

Behind me I heard a soft thump and I closed my eyes.

Joseph's laugh dissolved into a horrible gurgle and rasp.

"Get the key," I heard Shem say and there was a rustling.

"Zebulon," Tate said, his voice cracking.

"Let me see," I said to Ora and they released me, both of us turning back to see Joseph crumpled, his head slumped to one side, eyes closed as he bled from the stomach.

On the floorboards before him lay the prone body of the cat,

Zeb, the glowing amulet seeming to adhere to his stomach and seep into his fur.

I went to my knees to cradle the cat in my hands. His body was warm and I could feel his breathing, fast.

"He's still alive," I said.

"Get back," Ezra said. "Get top side. We have to dispose of the traitor."

I gathered Zeb to my chest and hurried up the stairs out onto the deck, careful not to touch the amulet myself. My eyes blurred with tears.

It was bad enough Joseph betrayed us. Bad enough he seemed to want to target me with that thing. But now a poor, innocent cat has taken the blow for me?

It's not fair.

For the next while, I just held Zeb to me. He seemed to know I was there, he butted his head weakly against my chest, before he fell asleep.

He lay in my arms with his paws curled up, his belly exposed where the magical amulet seemed to absorb into his body. I sat against the mast thinking I'd be out of the way there. Ora settled beside me.

"What's it going to do? The amulet, the magic, it's going inside him, what can it mean?" I asked Ora. My breath hitched, I was half sobbing.

Ora shook their head. "I don't know... I'm sorry, I've never seen any magic like this."

The crew came above deck slowly, Sagorika too, looking as if they'd awoken from a long sleep.

Tate and Ezra carried Joseph's limp body up, over to the side of the ship and tossed him into the sea without ceremony.

My heart hurt.

I'm sure if it hadn't been for Solomon's influence, Joseph could've still been alive. He wasn't a bad man, from the little I knew of him. Solomon had come to him in the night and swayed his will. Now it should have been me under the influence of whatever dark magic he had welded in Solomon's name.

Ora slipped their arm around me and held me while I held the unconscious cat.

Sagorika crouched in front of me. She eyed Ora, a question in her eyes, but she seemed to set it aside for the matter closer at hand.

"Let me see him," she said, gently, and reached to touch Zeb's paw.

I held him out to her and she hummed, looking him over. "We can put him in the infirmary, in my rooms," she said. "I'll do what I can for him. I have some herbs, some charms. Perhaps he can be saved."

"Please," I said. "If I can, I'd like to help."

For the next hour, Ora, Sagorika and I worked in her rooms.

We blended herbs and Sagorika crushed them into a paste with a mortar and pestle, we wrapped the spot the amulet had touched with leaves and ointment.

Finally, Ora chanted something over the body, in some strange language I assumed must be what they spoke under the waves. Sagorika held my hand as we watched this and I squeezed it tight, grateful for the reassurance offered.

When Ora had finished Zeb yawned, curled into a ball and started purring.

"That's a very good sign, I think," Sagorika said. "Nothing to do now but let him sleep it off."

CHAPTER TWENTY-EIGHT - IN WHICH ARRANGEMENTS ARE SETTLED UPON

We went back up on deck. The ship was sailing fast now, the mainsail full as we sped away from the Splintered Isles.

I realised, as the sun warmed my shoulders, that I'd been shirtless this entire time. How strange a thing not to notice.

Worse. Ora had no trousers on, still.

"We need to get you some clothes," I said, elbowing them.

"I have clothes," they said. They pulled the coat closer around themself.

"Something to cover your genitals," I said. I tugged at the waistband of my own trousers, but Ora pulled a face.

"I'd rather something like Sagorika was wearing, that looks more comfortable."

"A skirt? Well, why not?" I said. I turned around to find Sagorika nearby, eyeing Ora with interest. "Sagorika, have you anything you could loan?"

Sagorika nodded. "You're welcome to anything in my wardrobe, handsome." She gave Ora a wink that they returned readily.

I felt joy bubbling in my chest, but I knew there was another matter to be settled, and I didn't want to wait to do it.

Soon enough, I knew, I would need to sleep for a very long time. My muscles ached, and my bones felt tired, but I was able to hold off my exhaustion for a while longer.

"Let's do clothes in a moment," I said, taking Ora's hand.

I went to find Ezra, who was giving instructions to Shem at the helm.

"Ezra, a word if I may?" I asked, back to my old politeness due to the gravity of the conversation I wanted to have.

He nodded, unsurprised, and followed Ora and I to Tate's cabin. I knocked and pushed the door open. Tate looked up. He was shirtless and in the middle of washing himself with water and a cloth.

"To what do I owe...?" he looked at all three of us as Ezra closed the door. "All of this company?"

"We need to talk," I said.

"Right," Tate set his cloth back in the bowl and set it to one side. "Take a seat then, everyone."

Ezra pulled the desk chair out and settled on that. Tate sat on his bed, and I nodded to Ora to sit beside him.

I remained standing, trying to gather my thoughts. In the centre of the room like I was about to start reciting poetry.

I know what I want, and that's not to choose. My heart swells when I see every single one of these men, and I don't want to lose any of that. Besides, all the touching and kissing is absolutely delicious.

"Here's the thing," I said, by way of starting. "I don't want just one of you." Tate shifted, eyeing Ezra. I swallowed and hurried on. "I know it sounds impossible, and strange, and beyond anything polite society would find seemly, but I don't... I find that I don't care about that now. I want to be with all of you."

There, I said it.

Ezra shifted in his chair and then looked at Ora. Ora smiled at me guilelessly and nodded, as if it were the easiest thing in the world. Perhaps things like this happened all the time with merfolk?

Tate cleared his throat. "It won't be easy, lad, but... I find I have no objection, myself. Besides a certain, trepidation about having a merman on board."

"Folk," said Ora. "I'm not actually a man. I'm merfolk."

"Oh," Tate said. He nodded, but his eyebrows drew together heavily.

"Ora is..." I hesitated trying to articulate exactly how I felt about Ora. Like my soul had recognised them, perhaps. Or that they were another part of me.

The idea of being without them was preposterous, like suggesting I leave one of my arms behind. "Ora is non-negotiable. Well, I mean, unless you don't want to stay?" I went to Ora and took their hand, they squeezed it back instantly.

"I want to stay," they said easily. "You're the most interesting thing I've ever come across, and I want to learn more about the world up here. This big boat thing is fascinating, and the people on it, too."

I leaned in and kissed their forehead, grateful. Then turned to Tate and Ezra.

"Well, Ezra, you haven't spoken yet?" I said, my heart in my throat.

He looked between the three of us, then his face broke into a wide smile. "It's absolutely crazy, but damn, Gideon. If anyone could make it work, it'd be you."

Relief flooded me so hard I thought my knees would give out.

"Oh, thank the lord," I said. "I just... Honestly, I'm in love with all of you, and the idea of choosing just one is, well, it's impossible. I couldn't do it."

Tate laughed and took my hand, tugging me towards him.

"Hell, I've known Ezra long enough, and that sex we had was damn hot." He reached his other hand out to Ora. "Just need to get to know you better..."

"Ora of the Green Kelp Clan," Ora said, happily. They shifted onto their knees and shuffled closer. I turned and offered my hand to Ezra.

"Come here, you," I said, smiling. The relief had rapidly turned to excitement and anticipation.

I couldn't believe my luck, I had asked for what I wanted and they had all agreed. I was the luckiest boy on the seven seas.

Ezra stood and took my hand. "You're giving the orders now, are you?" He asked, one eyebrow arched as he pressed against my back. "You have to earn that with me, laddie."

"Just that order," I murmured, leaning back against him.

He wrapped an arm around my chest and leaned down to kiss my neck. My eyes half closed with pleasure, but I wanted to watch as Tate gently stripped my coat off Ora and Ora ran their hands over Tate's chest.

God, but they're all so beautiful, and so attractive together.

I stepped forward to the bed, pulling Ezra with me. He let go of me to pull his shirt off and I reached down to undo my trousers and kick them away, going to my knees on the bed. Ezra pulled his trousers off and moved close enough for me to plant kisses on his stomach and hip, teasing down to his cock, which stood out from him, hard and ready.

I watched, pressing my temple against his abdomen as he reached to play with Tate's hair, as I kissed his cock.

Tate groaned, pulling Ora tight against his chest, the two of them breathing heavily, Ora's hand pressed between them, stroking one or both of them.

Ora's hip pressed against mine, and I snaked a hand around their waist, my fingers playing on their skin as I took Ezra's cock into my mouth.

Ezra moaned appreciatively and I felt his hand in my hair, winding it around his hand and tugging gently. I braced my free hand around his waist, holding myself steady, because with all the pleasure and promise of more to come, I was almost lightheaded.

I opened my eyes to look sideways at Tate and Ora kissing deeply, and groaned around Ezra, licking him more frantically as my own need rose. He tugged me off him with his hand in my hair, and guided me towards them.

So generous, I thought. *Despite our earlier conversation some part of me wasn't sure if Ezra would really share...*

Ora turned instinctively to kiss me and Ezra let go of my hair, leaned in and kissed Tate.

Ora lay back on the bed, drawing me on top of him, and I went willingly, reaching a hand out to one of the others, not sure if it mattered which, but urging them to lie down as well. Ora parted their legs and I pressed against them, my own cock had barely been touched, and now I couldn't help but push inside them. The bed shifted, and Tate moved up to settle himself with one knee at either side of Ora's head.

Ora leaned up to lick under his balls and Tate made a high pitched and delightful noise of pleasure.

Behind me, I felt Ezra's hands, slicked with oil, teasing at my hole and I had to stop moving altogether - let him work so that I didn't just come on the spot and finish things almost before we'd started. Ora's chin tipped and his tongue flicked out and Tate moaned again. I leaned up as best I could, Tate leaned down and we kissed deeply.

His tongue plunged into my mouth and the familiar taste of him filled me with blissful desire.

Tate, my Tate. And my Ora, and my Ezra.

Is this really happening? Can I truly be this lucky? I can't possibly deserve this...

But any uncertainty I had was short lived. Underneath me, Ora rocked his hips and at the same moment Ezra pushed inside me and I cried out in sheer pleasure.

"So good," Tate groaned. His hand reaching to stroke Ora as I rolled my hips forward to fill them completely. Ora's hand reached behind me to grip Ezra's hip and pull him tighter in and I saw stars for a moment, my breath caught in my throat.

Ezra chuckled and leaned in, pressing me deeper into Ora until both of us were moaning. Tate moved his hips forward, I moved my head up a little and licked the tip of his cock.

There was a hand in my hair, now, and I had no idea whose it was - it didn't matter - another hand, I was sure this one was Ezra's, closed gently around my throat. I bucked my hips forward and then back, gratified at the pleasured noises I heard from first Ora and then Ezra.

My own pleasure pulsed at me, every part of my body seemed to be revelling in the multitude of touches.

I sucked Tate's cock into my mouth and groaned. As he rocked his hips I caught a glimpse of Ora's hand between his legs, teasing him with their fingers. Tate was groaning loud enough it echoed off the walls of the cabin.

I couldn't hold back. Ezra's hand tightened on my throat and I started to thrust my hips more violently, forwards and back, for there was incredible pleasure from both sides. Ezra pumped his hips, crashing against me with a loud slapping noise.

I felt Ora flood with warm liquid around my cock.

Is it that secretions thing they mentioned? Does it mean they're self lubricating somehow? I didn't know they could do that, I thought distantly.

He squeezed around my cock so hard I clenched around Ezra and in the same moment Tate bucked half down my throat and came.

With a rough thrust that had both Ora and myself crying out, Ezra filled me.

The orgasm that ripped through me then was so intense every muscle in my body tensed and released. I forgot how to breath, even as I swallowed down Tate's seed. My hands gripped the bed clothes and Ora's shoulder, as if I had to hold tight to the world or I'd fly off it.

I closed my eyes and felt as if I were sailing through the stars, detached from my body on a perfect wave of sensation.

Opening my eyes as the intensity of it faded, I gasped for breath. The hand had fallen from my throat and was now stroking my back. Tate's cock pressed against my lips, and I kissed it on instinct, although I could tell it was softening.

"That was marvellous," Ora murmured faintly, from somewhere below me.

Tate moaned his agreement and Ezra huffed out a word that could have been 'obviously'.

I whined despite myself as Ezra withdrew from me. I didn't want this all to end... but also, I wasn't sure my arms could hold me up any longer, so I lay fully down on Ora's chest.

Ora wrapped an arm around me as Ezra and Tate shifted, one to each side of us, and soon I was at the centre of a tangle of hot, sweaty limbs, and I had never felt more at peace with the world.

"I think I'm going to pass out," I muttered into Ora's chest. Three different hands petted my back and head. "But first."

With the last of my strength, I leaned over to kiss Tate, then turned to kiss Ezra and finally Ora. I was still inside Ora, come to think of it, but neither of us seemed to be worried about it.

That done, I submitted to the petting, the soothing hands, rested my head on Ora's shoulder and let sleep take me.

CHAPTER TWENTY-NINE - IN WHICH OUR STORY COMES TO AN END, FOR NOW

I woke up a little when Ora shifted out from under me, and there was another movement, but I just snuggled onto my side, curled up and drifted back to sleep.

It was a few hours later when I woke. The ship was quiet and it was dark outside the window. Ora was lying nearby on their front, watching me with a soft smile.

I smiled at them, reached a hand out to brush a curl back from their face. They were so damn gorgeous.

"Do you sleep?" I asked, my voice scratchy.

"Yeah, obviously, it's just a bit harder up here. I like this thing though." They picked up a bit of blanket and rubbed it between their fingers. "So soft."

"Yeah, blankets are pretty good." I smiled. Something had occurred to me as I slept and I wanted to allay a fear that had bubbled up. Even though I wasn't sure I was ready for their answer. "Are you really positive that you want to stay up here with me? Don't you have family and friends down, uh, down by the Islands? Under the ocean there, I mean."

Ora nodded, frowning a little. "But they'll still be there when

I come back," they said. "Merfolk live a long time, much longer than humans. I want to stay with you for now." They leaned up on their elbow and kissed me softly.

I felt a warmth spreading through my chest.

That's one thing sorted out then. There were a few difficult conversations still to have.

"Let's get you back to Sagorika for some clothes," I said. "We'll go to my room first for my clothes too..."

Once I had fresh trousers and a shirt on I felt more ready for what I had to do. It was something I had learned from my mother: Never underestimate the power of clean clothes and a fresh outfit.

I dropped Ora off with Sagorika to go through her clothing and try things on, confident that once they got to know each other better they'd be fast friends.

I went to check on the sleeping Zeb, stroked his fur gently. He had stretched out on his side, his head resting on two large front paws.

"He seems to be fine," Sagorika said. She smiled at me from the corner of the room where she kept her clothing, where Ora was making happy noises as he pawed through the sea chests.

"I'm going to find Tate and Ezra," I said. "Have fun, both of you."

I went out onto the deck.

Tate was talking with Shem who was at the helm. I waited for Tate to notice me before I went close enough to hear them.

"Evening, Gideon," he said. He held his arm out to me and I tucked in underneath it, pressing against his warm side.

"How long did I sleep?" I asked, leaning my cheek against his chest and waving at Shem.

"Three hours," he said. He guided me away from the helm and to the stern of the ship. "How're you feeling?"

"Somewhat amazing," I said. "Somewhat concerned... I haven't told you who I really am, and I really ought to."

Tate's grip on me tightened briefly, then he let go of me to look me in the eyes. "All right, I should probably tell you that Solomon said something about that."

"He did?" I swallowed, remembering. "Yes, he knew who I was, and that ..." I trailed off. Best not get ahead of myself. "I'm Gideon Keene, my father is Governor Keene of Kingston, and Solomon said that my father has sent ships... he's searching for me."

Tate nodded and then looked out towards the ocean. He thought for a moment. I shifted from one foot to the other.

"I mean, it's not like the British Navy aren't interested in us anyway. It's just... they're not usually active about it."

"Solomon also said there were bounties."

I watched his profile, so I saw when he smiled, and my shoulders relaxed.

"Tate?" I asked, smiling myself. His amusement was infectious.

"If you've decided you want to stay on the ship, Gideon, then we're happy to have you. Hell, you're probably still not the most wanted person on board. Governor father, or no."

"Who's the most wanted. Is that Ezra?" I asked, thinking back to what Solomon had said again.

Tate frowned, raised his eyebrows and shrugged. "Probably, yes?"

"I want to stay on the ship," I said. I bumped against his side until he turned and I could slip my arms around his neck. "I want to stay with all of you."

"Very happy to hear it." He said, his voice cracked a little, and he leaned in to kiss me warmly. I melted into it, losing myself in the warmth of him.

Finally, he broke the kiss, and I was glad he'd wound his arms around my waist because I was in danger of falling down, my knees weak. Tate chuckled and held on tight, supporting me. Once I had my legs under me again he let go.

"What're you going to do right now?"

"I should talk to Ezra, too," I said. "Do you know where he is?"

"Below deck I think," he said. "You should make sure you get some dinner as well, there'll be leftovers in the galley." He ruffled his hand through my hair and kissed my forehead. "You coming back to my room to sleep?"

"I hadn't thought," I said. "Maybe, I'll, I'll see what Ora wants to do. They did mention sleeping better under water. Is there... is there some way... ?"

"Maybe if we loosen the bowsprit netting some," he said, head tilting to the side. "We can look at it tomorrow. I like Ora," he added, winking at me. "Very interesting boy, that one."

"Not a boy, folk, or just Ora," I corrected. I went up on my toes to kiss his cheek, smiling at the feel of his beard against my face. "I love you, Tate."

"Love you, too, Gideon Keene," he said. "So um, what are the chances I could borrow another of those romance stories you have in your cabin? The one I read was so sweet, and I want more."

I swallowed a surprised laugh and nodded.

I wouldn't have predicted he'd be interested, but it would be nice to have someone to discuss the plots with.

"Help yourself." Sighing happily I went below deck in search of Ezra.

I found Ezra napping on his hammock in the crew sleeping area. His boots and outer layers were off and he looked surprisingly soft and sweet asleep in only his black shirt and trousers.

Is it taking my life in my hands if I wake him up?

I leaned over and kissed him softly on the mouth.

He woke up instantly, tensing under me and flailing his limbs enough that he rolled out of his hammock and landed on the floor.

I couldn't help but laugh as he scrambled to his feet, his cheeks flushed.

"Right. Gideon. Hello," he said. He shoved a hand through his hair and stood up straighter. I swallowed the laughter.

"Hello," I said. "How are you?"

"A little bruised, now." He smiled then, reached a hand out and tugged me towards him by the waistband of my trousers. I kissed him happily, my heart was so full and happy from all these kisses and touches. It felt like I had made up for a lifetime of longing in the last week or so, and I was more contented than I'd ever been.

"I wanted to check in with you," I said. "I know you're somewhat... possessive." Finally, I was blushing again. But this time it wasn't because I was embarrassed at the thought of sex, but flushing with pleasure at the thought of the things Ezra might do to me. And how much I wanted to try things out.

"I can be," Ezra said. "And I will definitely want to have some alone time with you."

"Of course," I said. "I want that too."

"And I cannot *believe* that you not only made friends with a member of the merfolk, but you brought him - them - *on board* with us. Have you no idea what the stories say about their kind? How dangerous they can be?"

I shrugged some. "They only eat people who would die anyway, people who fall overboard..."

Ezra shook his head and sighed, pulling his hair back again. "You're impossible," he said. "I'm going to have to spend some time training you."

"So, you're all right with the arrangement? I know you were the least ready to accept it," I swallowed, a little nervous.

"I'm all right," he said. "Tate is like a gorgeous mountain I always wanted to climb."

That surprised a laugh out of me. "Wonderful. Um, what... I have to ask, what does training involve?"

"You'll find out, pet," he said. He yanked on my pants again and I stumbled against him, my hands going to his chest to catch myself. "And if you're very good and obedient, you'll enjoy it a lot."

"R-right," I said, breathless.

"And if you're naughty or disobedient, then we'll explore your limits for enduring pain."

He kissed me then, one of those signature Ezra kisses that felt like a battle I was happy to lose. My blood pumped hot through my veins and I moaned softly into his mouth.

"I'll probably continue to sleep alone, though," Ezra said. "Just in case you thought we'd all move into the Captain's cabin. I like alone time. And I sleep far better on a hammock than a soft bed."

I nodded and kissed his cheek. "That's fine, as long as I can sleep beside you every now and then."

He nodded, let his hand slip down my back and squeezed my bottom. Then he slapped it. "As you wish."

I jolted against him and kissed him one more time.

"Tomorrow then," I said.

"Mmhm," he let go of me and slapped my rear again, making me gasp. "Sleep well, pet."

I went back up to my cabin and sat on the small bed, taking a moment to myself. My eyes landed on the miniature portrait of my mother. She smiled at me, and although rationally I knew this was the same expression she had always had, tonight it looked as if she were proud of me.

As if she approved.

I explained the past few days to her, and sighed happily as I got to details of the arrangement.

"We're all going to be together," I said. "I know it's like nothing you've ever heard of, Mama, but they make me happy, and I honestly think I can make them happy, too. Assuming, that is, they don't all change their minds."

I was giving her a kiss when I heard a scratching at the door to my cabin.

"Zeb!" I jumped up and opened the door, looking down expecting to see the familiar black fuzzy face looking back up at me.

Instead I saw large, bare, men's feet.

I looked slowly up, taking in tight black leather pants, and a torn grey shirt worn open with the sleeves rolled up.

He was almost as tall as Tate, and his face was weirdly familiar. His skin was a beautifully warm, deep brown and he had a ragged scar across the bridge of his nose. As I gazed at him, I saw the upper shell of his right ear was missing a chunk. There was another scar just above his left eye. His eyes were a startling deep green. The green of seaweed. They were large and open, and as I gazed at him, I realised I knew those eyes. But where from?

"Let me in," he said, loudly.

"I uh, who are you?" I asked.

The man pushed past me roughly and climbed onto the bed, settling awkwardly and trying to fold his legs underneath him. "Zeb," he said, as if it should be obvious.

My mouth dropped open.

Zeb? The cat? Why was he a human now? He was certainly taking possession of my bed as if he was Zeb. But how was this possible?

Sagorika appeared in the doorway. "Sorry, Gideon, I couldn't stop him," she said, breathless, her eyes wide.

"I'm... what? What happened?" I asked. My heart was thudding dully - I didn't think I could be surprised by anything after the last few days but here we were.

Ora leaned into the doorway as well, their face bright and smiling. "The magic made him into this," he said.

"We're not exactly sure how," Sagorika said. "Near as I can tell the amulet was a transformation curse, but maybe Ora's magic made it less... dangerous?"

"Zeb?" I asked, turning back to the handsome man on my bed.

"Gideon," he said. "Do you have any fish? I'm starving."

"N-not in here," I said. "Maybe in the galley, are you *really* Zeb?"

I walked closer to him and gazed into his face. He looked

back at me with a tired expression. "Of course I am. I always sleep in here. You're my human."

"I'm your..." I trailed off as Ora laughed behind me.

"He's a lot of people's human, actually," they said.

"Mm." Zeb looked at Ora, unimpressed. "You smell like fish."

"I think I'd better get Tate..." Sagorika said.

"Yes, get Tate," Zeb said. "He's been completely stupid about a number of things. Especially about you, Gideon. Ezra too, what fools."

"Zeb, we've..." I trailed off. "Well, you were asleep, but we've come to a sort of agreement."

He shook his head and lifted his hand to his mouth, licked the back of it and then frowned and dropped his hand back down.

I sat beside him on the end of the bed. "Um, aren't you disturbed about being a human now?"

Zeb shook his head. "No, this is fine. And now I can tell you all how you're being stupid, so actually, it's pretty good."

"Right," I said. I went to stand up again but Zeb caught hold of my hand and pulled me back.

"Kiss me?" he said.

"I don't know about that," I said. Even though Zeb was remarkably handsome, the fact that he had recently been a cat was disconcerting.

"I do," he said. I looked over at Ora who was leaning against the doorframe in a flowing pink skirt and a white shirt, their arms crossed, and softly laughing to themself.

No help there.

"I know you better than any of these fools," he said. He leaned closer and I caught my breath. He smelled incredible, like sunshine and warmth. "All those nights of you unloading

192

your soul, I remember all of it, and I understand. You and I have already slept together how many times?"

"Not like this," I breathed.

"What's going on?" Tate asked from outside.

Zeb's hand tightened on my forearm and I looked helplessly at the Captain. "I think... I think we have a complication," I said.

.... To be continued.

Preorder book two: First Mate's Pet

If you enjoyed this book, please consider leaving a review on Amazon. Indie authors rely on star ratings and reviews to go up the algorithm and be seen by more readers. Even one sentence will help ☺

Sign up for my newsletter for exclusive content and updates on new releases
https://www.subscribepage.com/q4c4n0

Come and visit Drake online:
Facebook: https://www.facebook.com/drake.lamarque.3
Facebook reader's group: https://www.facebook.com/groups/1272511269588779/
Twitter: https://twitter.com/DrakeLamarque
Pinterest: https://www.pinterest.nz/drakelamarque/
Newsletter: https://www.subscribepage.com/q4c4n0

BOOK TWO OF HIS PIRATICAL HAREM – FIRST MATE'S PET

Buy Now

Things were looking good, until the ship's cat became a man...

I didn't mean to join a pirate ship, but now that I'm here, well. Life is pretty good. Between the sexy and intimidating Captain Tate, the mysterious First Mate, Ora the merfolk and now Zeb the ship's cat I'm well entertained.

Rumours abound that the Royal Navy are searching for me at my father's order, and between that, an eventful trip to Tortuga (the famed pirate town) and maintaining the relationships with the crew... I've certainly got my work cut out for me.

Meet the crew:

Gideon: a well bred young man who is discovering his forbidden desires aren't necessarily a problem at sea

Tate: the impressive Captain with a sweet side

Ezra: the controlling and alluring First Mate

Ora: a genderqueer, sweet and mystical merman

Zeb: a cat shifter, who's learning about being human

MM romance, this is part two of a multiple book series - working towards a HEA at the end of the series

BOOK THREE OF HIS PIRATICAL HAREM – MERFOLK'S MATE

Buy Now

The British Navy caught up to the Grey Kelpie, and everything I'd built for my life has fallen apart.

Tate and Ezra are headed for the gallows. Ora has disappeared into an unwelcome sea and I have no idea what's become of the ship's cat...

It's up to me to save them, but I'm trapped on the Naval ship, the same as my lovers. If I'm to get us out of here, I'm going to have to use all my wits, and maybe a little magic?

Meet the crew:

Gideon: a well-bred young man discovering a new side of himself

Tate: the sweet Captain with a dark past

Ezra: a dominating First Mate who's slowly finding his soft side

Ora: a mystical merfolk who understands more than the rest

Zeb: an affectionate cat shifter who knows what he wants

MM romance, this is part three of a multiple book series - working towards a HEA at the end of the series - cannot be read as a standalone.

Content warning: some knife and blood play in one scene.

Rival Princes by Jaxon Knight

There are three golden rules for new recruits at Fairyland
Theme Park:

1. No breaking character, even if you're dying of heat exhaustion
    2. Always give guests the most magical time
    3. No falling in love.

Nate's only been at work one day, and he's already broken all
three.

Fast-tracked into a Prince role, Nate's at odds with Dash, the
handsome not-so-charming prince who is supposed to be
training him. Nate doesn't know how he ended up on Dash's bad
side, but the broody prince sure is hot when he gets mad.

Dash has worked long and hard to play Prince Justice at
Fairyland. Now, instead of focusing on his own performance, he

is forced to train newbie Nate to be the perfect prince. Nate's annoying ease with the guests coupled with his charm and good looks could dethrone Dash from his number one spot ... so why does he secretly want to kiss him?

Fairyland heats up as sparks fly between the two rival princes. Will they get their fairytale romance before they're kicked out of Fairyland for good?

Find out in this standalone MM contemporary romance by Jaxon Knight, set in an amusement park where fairytales can come true.

ALSO PUBLISHED BY GREY KELPIE STUDIO

Mischief and Mayhem by Jaxon Knight

Mischief

Protecting royalty at Fairyland theme park seemed about as far from Afghanistan as Cody could get. But the hot new rollercoaster brings up some unexpected trouble - and not the kind of trouble he knows how to handle alone.

Mayhem

Dean loves running the Spaceship Mayhem roller coaster - he gets to meet new people every day! When he sees a handsome, troubled security guard repeatedly fail to ride it, he sees an opportunity to help. And maybe they can be more than friends?

Cody reluctantly accepts cute, boy-next-door Dean's help and sparks fly between them, but between mischief, mayhem and miscommunication, can they ever make a relationship work?

Mischief and Mayhem is a slow burn, opposites attract MM sweet romance featuring snark, foolishness, motorbikes, assumptions, the chicken door and a HEA

Recipe for Chaos by Jaxon Knight

The recipe is simple:
  Charlie cooks an amazing meal
  Charlie impresses heir to the theme park Max Jones
  Charlie gets a promotion and a dash of control over his
kitchen

But the perfect recipe becomes unpalatable with one wrong
ingredient and Max Jones is not behaving how Charlie
expected...

Max is meant to inherit the entire Fairyland theme park but he
just wants to party, have fun and bed as many people as possible.
That is, until he meets Charlie and falls for him so hard he can't
even finish the delicious meal.

Charlie doesn't have time for clubs or helicopter flights over the city, but Max is accustomed to getting what he wants, and he wants Charlie.

Featuring one part Billionaire, one part sensible chef, six cups of attraction, a generous dose of snark and a freshly prepared Happy Ever After.

ALSO PUBLISHED BY GREY KELPIE STUDIO

The Good, the Bad, and the Dad by Jaxon Knight

Haru is a single dad, a widower, doing his best to balance his career and raising his little girl, Minako. Thankfully Fairyland theme park is a haven for both of them. However, when both a prince and a pirate start courting Haru, his balancing act gets a lot harder...

Cillian plays a pirate at Fairyland theme park and he loves playing the rogueish character in and out of work hours. The last thing he wants is to settle down with a guy with a kid, so can't he stop thinking about handsome single dad Haru. And why can't he stop looking at pictures of Prince Magnificence and his stupid symmetrical face? And why does he keep running into both of them?

Grayson feels he's found his home in the role of Prince Magnificence, but he's more likely to run from love than seek it out. Until he meets Haru, that is. Christmas is complicated by

Grayson's role being featured in a special Christmas celebration. Not only that, but his feelings for Haru, and his possible rival Cillian keep on growing. Maybe it's time to stop hiding who he really is?

--

The Good, the Bad and the Dad is a sweet MMM romance featuring a single father, a rogue and a trans prince with a heart of gold. No cheating, just the tentative first steps into polyamory.